the music thief

the
music thief

peni r. griffin

Henry Holt and Company - New York

Henry Holt and Company, LLC
Publishers since 1866
115 West 18th Street
New York, New York 10011
www.henryholt.com

Henry Holt is a registered trademark of Henry Holt and Company, LLC
Copyright © 2002 by Peni R. Griffin
Distributed in Canada by H. B. Fenn and Company Ltd.

Library of Congress Cataloging-in-Publication Data
Griffin, Peni R. The music thief / Peni R. Griffin

p.   cm.

Summary: Living in San Antonio, Texas, eleven-year-old Alma tries to cope with the
drive-by shooting death of her favorite Latina singer, as well as deal with the struggles
of her various family members, and finds herself doing something she knows is wrong.

[1. Conduct of life—Fiction. 2. Family problems—Fiction. 3. Family
life—Texas—Fiction. 4. Hispanic Americans—Fiction. 5. Music—Fiction.
6. Gangs—Fiction. 7. San Antonio (Tex.)—Fiction.] I. Title.

PZ7.G88136 Mu 2002   [Fic]—dc21   2002024089

ISBN 0-8050-7055-9 / First Edition—2002 / Designed by Donna Mark
Printed in the United States of America on acid-free paper. ∞

1   3   5   7   9   10   8   6   4   2

For Carmen "T" the mosquito and all the poderitos

—P. R. G.

the music thief

- 1 -

the *letter*

The day after school let out, Alma put the new Jovita tape into her player on low volume, so as not to wake her baby niece, and wrote a letter. She sat sideways at the changing table, the paper springy between her felt-tip pen and the vinyl cushion, while Silvita napped in the fluttery shadow of the curtains. Alma wrote with none of her usual frowning difficulty. Jovita wasn't a teacher. She would understand a letter that slid between English and Spanish in midsentence, like the ordinary speech of most people Alma knew. The only problem was to make Jovita feel the way Alma wanted her to feel.

Alma wrote her letter in Spanglish, but in English it would have said:

Dear Jovita,

You are the greatest singer in the world, and I am proud that you live in my town. Even though you live on the south side and I live closer to the middle, I am still proud because it is all San Antonio. I am listening to my tape of your new album, and it is the best album I have ever heard. Your other albums are good, too, but this is the best. I can't play your music loud because it would wake up my niece, Silvita. She lives in my room since my grandmother died. My grandmother would let me play your music as much as I wanted, but babies need sleep. Abuela and I would play your music real loud, and she wanted for us to play "La florita" at her funeral, but Mama said we shouldn't play dance music at a funeral. I don't know why not if it was what Abuela wanted. She liked the parts about the flowers coming back every year.

Someday I will be a singer like you and play instruments with a band and maybe be famous. Or maybe I will just play for people to dance to my songs. As long as I play music, that's the main thing. I can almost read music, they taught us the notes on a little recorder at school, but I know it is hard work and you have to have an instrument and practice a lot. My brother, Eddie, used to play saxophone in band and he practiced all the time and never sounded right. Lalo, my sister's husband, showed me some chords on his accordion, but he had to sell it when Silvita was born. Eddie says girls don't make good musicians, but you are proof he doesn't know what he's talking about. Lalo says if you work hard enough you can do what you want to do, and he's right, because you did. I am eleven and will start middle school in the fall. They don't teach accordion at middle school, but maybe I can learn guitar or something.

The title cut on your album is coming on and I wish I could turn it up, but Silvita is napping. All your songs are good, but "La luna de agosto" is the best one, and someday maybe I will hear you play it at a concert. I hope so.

Tu amiga,
Alma Perez

Alma chewed the pen's plastic cap and read this over. There was still a little room left at the bottom of the page. *P.S.,* she wrote, *School is over. This is not a school project. It's what I really truly feel in my heart and I wanted you to know.*

There! She was glad she'd put in the part about "in my heart," because *En mi corazón* had been her favorite song till Jovita's new album came out. She folded the paper neatly into thirds and went to the living room to find a stamp and an envelope.

Lalo was at the desk, copying his class notes, and Eddie slept on the couch. Alma hesitated, hovering behind her brother-in-law's chair. He didn't like to be disturbed while he was studying, but the mail would be here soon and she wanted to get the letter out today.

"What is it, Alma?" asked Lalo.

"I need a stamp and an envelope," she said. "I'm sorry."

Lalo opened the center drawer and passed them to her. "Writing to your boyfriend?"

Alma glanced over at Eddie. He *looked* asleep. "Jovita."

"That singer? Where you going to get her address?" Lalo leaned back in his chair and stretched.

"Out of the phone book," Alma said.

"A big star like her won't have a listed number. Better send it care of her record company."

"She'll be in the phone book, all right. Or anyway, her mama will be."

"But you don't know her mama's name."

"Do too. It's on the tape below the playlist. *A mi mamá, Lourdes Ramos de Aguilar.*" She pulled the battered white pages out from under the phone. "Here, I'll show you." Alma found her easily and held the page out to Lalo with her finger under the name. "See? And Jovita lives with her mother. I saw it on TV."

"Well, what do you know?" said Lalo. "If I was a big star, I sure wouldn't let everybody know where I was. And I wouldn't be living in that crummy part of town, either. I'd be out in the Dominion with the millionaires."

"But Jovita's not like that," Alma informed him proudly. "She's staying in the same neighborhood she grew up in, and fixing up her mama's house, and giving money to parks and community centers and things. 'Cause she's not all selfish and stuck-up like most rich people. She wants to make things better for her friends."

"Yeah, for her homeys," said Eddie, rolling over.

Alma glared at him. "Jovita doesn't have homeys!"

"Does too," said Eddie. "And you know it. It was on the same TV show. Your perfect Jovita is one of Las Howling Madres."

"She is not!" yelled Alma. "She left the gang ages and ages ago! You take that back right now!"

"People don't leave gangs, except in a box," said Eddie. "Gangs are your family."

"Only if you're a loser," Lalo replied. "Gangs're kid stuff. And speaking of loser kid stuff, where were you last night?"

"None of your business," growled Eddie. "You're not my brother."

"I am now," said Lalo.

Alma hurriedly copied Jovita's mother's address onto the envelope and took it out to stick on the mailbox with the fistful of bills Mama had paid last night. Lalo and Eddie's argument about gangs veered into an argument about Eddie getting a job. Next door, Mrs. B.'s smallest cat, the gray tiger, stalked something, and Mrs. B. herself weeded her flower bed, singing some Anglo song about where all the flowers had gone, which made sense, because the flower bed didn't have as many flowers in it as it had when Mr. B. was alive.

Alma shied away from the thought. Thinking about dead Mr. B. was almost like thinking about her dead grandmother, and she didn't want to.

It was bad enough that Silvita's crib took up the same corner of the room as Abuela's bed had; that the changing table replaced Abuela's rocking armchair. She didn't need to remember how she and Abuela used to sit out here in the evenings, eating *paletas* and listening to the radio or to Mrs. B. playing piano next door. *Paletas* were frozen fruit juice on a stick, and Alma never ate one faster than it could melt down her arms. Mr. B. would be working in his yard, and he would wave at them when he came out and again when he went back in. Eddie would play touch football in the street with the boys that used to live on the corner, using the oak trees between the sidewalks and the curbs as yard markers and goals. Rosalia would practice cheers with her friend Marisol. When the radio played a really good number, Abuela would teach the girls and Eddie the *baile,* kicking off her flip-flops to dance barefoot on the dusty drive.

The long twilights were perfect and whole in Alma's head. No matter how hard she tried, she could not shut her brain down fast enough to keep herself from remembering all of them and feeling the stab in her chest that was the knowledge there wouldn't be any more.

Way in the back of the house, Silvita started crying. Mama and Rosalia were at their weekend jobs; Lalo needed to finish his note copying and get ready for his weekend job. Eddie always acted as if Silvita didn't exist. Alma hurried inside, thinking how pleased Jovita would be to get her letter.

- 2 -

the news

Alma brought Silvita to the breakfast table with her Tuesday morning. "Yeah, sure, I guess I see," Lalo was saying to Rosalia, "but did you have to blow off the whole job because of that?"

"*Yes,*" said Rosalia. "Why are you so uptight? You want me to put up with crud like that all day?"

"No, it's just—your mama's working herself to death here, and Eddie's not doing nothing, and my delivering pizza at night and stocking on weekends doesn't help much. And if we can't cover the bills, I'll have to quit school, and I'll never get a good job and it'll all go down the tubes."

"Chill, will you? I'll get another job in a day or two. A better one than flipping burgers, you watch.

Meantime"—she stretched out her arms to Silvita with a dazzling smile—"I get to spend the whole day with my little girl! *Hola, bebé!* You got a kiss for your mama?"

Silvita kicked and gurgled as Alma handed her over and fetched tortillas and eggs off the stove, flipping on the radio above the sink as she passed. The last bars of *"En mi corazón"* were just fading away, followed by the opening ones of *"La luna de agosto."* "Morning, Alma," said Lalo. "You're up with the birds."

"Silvita wouldn't let me sleep," said Alma. "What happened with the job?"

"I don't want to go over it all *again*," Rosalia said. "The manager was a jerk, that's all. We walked out in the middle of the shift, Marisol and me, and we went to the arcade for a while to cool off." She yawned. "But you should be glad, 'cause you don't have to baby-sit today."

Alma sat down with her breakfast. "Is that Tino asleep on the floor in the living room?" she asked.

"Sí," said Lalo. "Don't ask me what it's about. I only live here. If Mama hadn't said not to, I'd throw him out."

Alma agreed with the part of her mind that wasn't listening to the music, but Rosalia said: "Shame on you! You know his father beats him!"

"I know he *says* his father beats him," said Lalo. "The only thing I know about Tino for sure is I've seen him hanging with Los Chupacabras. Remember last year at school? I don't see how a gangster wanna-be can do Eddie any good."

"Maybe Tío Eddie can do Tino some good, hmm, Silvita?" Rosalia tickled Silvita's belly with her nose, and Silvita giggled and clutched at her hair. Already she had a much longer reach than a month ago. Sometimes lately Alma thought she could see her growing. When Rosalia had first come home from the hospital, taking care of Silvita had seemed almost like playing baby dolls to Alma, but she was too big and wiggly for that now. Rosalia still looked more like a big sister than a mother, though.

Lalo glanced at the clock and shoveled down eggs at double speed. Alma dawdled over hers. It was earlier than she'd wanted to get up, but once Silvita woke up, she banged on the bars of the crib till you took her out. The radio finished *"La luna de agosto,"* and Jovita started singing the one about dancing till the sun came up. Alma tapped her feet under the table. Rosalia played with Silvita. Lalo watched them with the expression reserved for them: half fond, half nervous. Alma yawned, glad the DJ had decided to play three Jovita songs, one from each album, in a row, but wishing he'd waited till she got out here to start.

Lalo scooted back his chair, drained his coffee mug, and wiped his mouth. "We got three tests and two labs today, can you believe it?" He dropped kisses onto Silvita and Rosalia, flinching when the baby grabbed at his nose, scooped up his bag lunch, and hurried out, leaving his plate on the table. Usually Lalo was good about cleaning up after himself, but Alma could see where three tests and two labs would make him careless. A plane went by overhead, drowning out the end of the song. When it faded away, the DJ was talking, but not in his usual bright, enthusiastic DJ voice.

". . . in memory of our Jovita," he said.

Alma stopped with her tortilla halfway to the plate, her mouth frozen in midchew.

"You're Mama's little love bug, aren't you?" babbled Rosalia.

"I don't even know how to talk about this," said the DJ. "The police are saying it was a drive by, and I'm asking, who would—"

"*Ay, la niña más dulce del mundo!*"

"*Callate!*" Alma motioned for Rosalia to be quiet.

". . . an accident. But everyone knew her. She lived there her whole life. It was *her* neighborhood. So—"

"Don't you hush me," said Rosalia.

Alma leaped to her feet and ran to the radio. "I don't care! Just shut up!"

". . . don't see how they could do this. How anybody could do this! Jovita'd left all that gang stuff behind her, and—"

"Don't you talk to me that way."

Alma gasped for breath, feeling as if a rock the size of a basketball had landed in her stomach. "Listen! Just listen!"

". . . didn't regain consciousness. I guess we can be glad that she never knew what hit her. But that's not so much to be glad about."

Rosalia listened now. Silvita made half-formed noises, the same ones over and over: "Ta-ta-ta, ta-ta- ta."

"And all I've got to say is, the cops better get those *cholos* before her fans do!" The DJ sounded the way Alma felt. "I'm going to stop talking now and let you listen some more. Listen up good, because this is all that's left of our Jovita."

A heartbeat of silence. Another.

The *bajo sexto* kicked in. Alma recognized the first chord—"Not Anymore," the one about the girl who would never dance in the sun again because the drugs and the guns and the gangs took her away.

Alma felt the sound rising in her as Silvita gurgled and Rosalia looked blank. She didn't want to let the sound out. She wanted to be absolutely quiet and listen to Jovita sing.

"*Qué?*" asked Rosalia. "Did he say Jovita *died*? In a drive by? Is that what he said?"

The sound forced her mouth open as Jovita's full, perfect voice launched the first verse, and Alma heard nothing but her own crying, until Silvita started crying, too.

- 3 -

the *fight*

Once, in first grade, a bigger girl had beaten up Alma on the playground. She couldn't remember now what it had been about, but she'd soon stopped fighting back and collapsed into a ball, trying to wrap herself in a protective layer of arms and legs. All the air was kicked out of her stomach, her whole face collapsed under the force of fists like thrown cinder blocks, and her arms and legs shuddered with pain.

This was worse.

That time, just when Alma was sure she was going to die, Eddie had come along and torn the bigger girl off her. She could remember him washing her face and telling her it was okay, it was over, she was going to be fine.

No one could end this. She was not going to be fine.

When Abuela died, everyone said it was a release. She'd had a cancer, they said, and had been in pain and never mentioned it, probably because doctors cost so much. It was no good crying, they'd said, since she was happy, dancing with her old friends up in heaven. So Alma had swallowed, and swallowed, until she thought her throat would explode, and had not cried.

No one could pretend that this was a blessing in disguise.

Alma and Rosalia stayed by the radio, crying together and listening to Jovita's songs, interrupted by the occasional weather report, commercial, or discussion of the news.

Jovita had been walking to a friend's house when a car came by and opened fire.

She had been taken straight to the hospital with three—no, five—no, only two—bullets in her and died at 3 A.M.

So far the police had no leads, though everybody knew that a drive by meant gangs. They didn't know whether it was Jovita's old gang, Las Howling Madres, or their rivals, Las Princesas de Pain, or maybe a guy gang.

They didn't have a description of the car or of the people in it.

They didn't know whether Jovita had been the target or just been walking past a targeted house.

A four-year-old boy and a ninety-four-year-old woman inside the house had been wounded and all the front windows broken.

A teenager lived in the house, but she might or might not be in a gang.

The DJ, the weather guy, and the news lady all had ideas about what had happened, and people kept calling in with new rumors, but nobody really knew anything, and sooner or later they would always give up and play the music.

At ten-thirty, Rosalia chased Eddie and Tino out of the living room so she and Silvita could watch her *novela* on the TV. The boys slouched into the kitchen and helped themselves to leftover pizza out of the refrigerator. When Alma told them the news, Eddie's face got blank and pale, and he caught the counter with his hands, as if he'd lost his balance.

Then Tino snorted. "Served her right. She was probably going to squeal."

Alma couldn't talk for half a minute. "She *couldn't* squeal! She wasn't in the gang anymore!"

"Yeah, right," said Eddie, standing up straight again, but talking to the wall.

"Like she really would have stayed in that crummy neighborhood if it wasn't for her homeys," said Tino.

"She was trying to make it less crummy," protested Alma. "Don't you know anything?"

"Don't you know anything?" Eddie turned around at last, parroting her words back at her, then went on, in the sneering voice he used so often lately, especially around Tino. "Nobody does anything for anybody else. That's a story the rich people tell the poor people so the poor people don't take their stuff away. Jovita was getting rich enough to start pretending to help folks, that's all."

"But her homeys knew better," agreed Tino. "Maybe she wasn't going to squeal. Maybe she wouldn't share."

"Yeah. Yeah, she blew off her turn to buy the beer."

"All that money she had, she should've been buying *all* the beer!"

Tino and Eddie laughed above the sound of Jovita's happy voice singing *"La bamba."* Alma stood up and yelled, leaning on the table, into Eddie's face, "She's *dead*! How can you laugh when she's *dead*?"

"S'easy," Eddie mumbled around his mouthful of

pizza, his eyes skittering around in his face as if it hurt to look at anything. "Look, I'm all broken up. She was hot, and now I'll never get a date with her."

Tino hooted with laughter and slapped him on the back. "Good one, *vato*! I've had about as much of this as I can take. Let's get us a good station." He turned the tuning knob on the radio.

"Hey! I'm listening to that!" Alma jostled him aside.

"Not anymore you're not," said Tino, shoving her against the sink, pushing all the air out of her.

Alma bent over, tears pouring down her face.

"*Ay, vato,*" said Eddie, far away. She waited for him to say: "Leave my sister alone," or, "You can't push her around," or something else useful.

"The Spanish stations ain't going to play nothing but Jovita all day," Eddie said. "See if you can find some country."

Alma ran to her room and turned on her tape player, thumbing the volume control to maximum. The accordion solo from *"Solo para ti"* filled the room. Alma sat on the bed, staring at a picture of Abuela above the changing table. Abuela had hibiscus flowers in her long black hair and wore a swirling dance gown. "My firework dress," Abuela had called it, but every color in the picture had faded to shades of blue and white. She had won a dance competition at the community center, the same day she found out she was pregnant with Mama's brother, Manuel. The happiest day of her life.

Alma lay on her bed, the music holding her tight. From behind her shut lids, she pretended that the rocking chair still stood in the corner, that Abuela sat there listening and mourning, too. Mama said that Abuela watched them from heaven, but that wasn't close enough.

Had Jovita gotten her letter? Had she read it before the bullets ripped into her? Had she been planning how to answer as she walked to her friend's house through the hot June darkness? Or had she maybe been planning a new song, about a dark night in June, dancing home on a dark night in June, when the car screeched past and interrupted her forever?

Alma played all three tapes and started over. Whenever she had to turn one, she could hear the TV people talking about household cleansers, if they were in a commercial, or about who loved who, if they were part of a show. She heard Eddie and Tino talking about where they should hang out, about some girl or other, about what they should do to fix something that had gone down last night. She switched her tapes as fast as she could, curled up on the bed with her eyes shut.

After she turned on *"La luna de agosto,"* the door opened. "Hey, it's past lunchtime," said Rosalia. "You want some hot dogs?"

"I'm not hungry," said Alma to the ceiling.

Rosalia came in and sat down next to her. "You just going to lie here and listen to her all day?"

"There's nothing else to do."

"Hey, it's terrible. I'm upset, too. But you can't spend the rest of your life here." She laid her hand on Alma's head. "How about peanut butter?"

"I'm not *hungry.*" Alma jerked her head away.

Rosalia stood up, and her voice got hard. "Turn the music down and go eat! It's time for Silvita's nap."

Alma rolled off the bed and carried the tape player with her to the kitchen. Jovita's voice clashed with Garth Brooks's. Eddie and Tino ate pork rinds and drank beer. Had they been eating all this time? It was nearly two. "Lalo and Mama won't like you drinking up their beer," Alma said. "You're too young to drink, anyway."

"You mind your own business," mumbled Eddie around a pork rind, "and turn that tape off."

"You're not my boss."

"You let your little sister talk at you like that?" asked Tino.

"No," said Eddie, and yanked the player away from her.

Alma fought him for it, but he had three years and fifty pounds on her. All she got for her trouble was a broken fingernail. "You give that back! It's mine!"

"Is not," said Eddie, popping out the tape. "I bought it."

"You gave it to me when you bought your boom box."

"I *loaned* it to you. Now my boom box is on the fritz and I need this back." He tossed the tape at her head.

Alma caught it, glaring at him. "It's *mine!* You give it *back!*"

"Shut up!" yelled Rosalia down the hall as Silvita started to cry. "Now listen what you did!"

"Eddie's stealing from me!"

"I don't care if he's burning the house down—don't yell when I'm putting Silvita down for a nap!"

Clutching the precious tape, Alma stormed out and slammed the door.

- 4 -

the cat flap

The country music followed her through the open window. Her bike leaned against the porch, its broken chain dangling, useless. The unwatered grass hurt her bare feet. Along the fence, one of the roses of Sharon bloomed, but the other stood lifeless and pale. Shoving her tape into her shorts pocket, Alma hurled herself at the dead shrub, snapping off its papery twigs and branches. Soon even the main stem lay in a heap, and Alma felt no better. She leaned against the chain-link fence, sniffing and blinking.

Mrs. B.'s yard was green and shady. All her roses of Sharon bloomed, purple and crinkly as the gauze dress Jovita wore in the *"En mi corazón"* video. Alma gripped the fence and glared at the shaggy gray-and-white cat sprawled on Mrs. B.'s back steps. Long, long ago, all the houses on this street had looked much alike, rows of neat bungalows with deep eaves and wide porches. Now Alma's back porch was falling apart, with the remnants of a long-ago brown paint job and several rotten boards, but Mrs. B.'s had been enclosed with a screen and the trim and steps painted green the summer before Mr. B. died. You could tell rent houses from owned houses on this street because the rent houses looked more or less like Alma's and the owned houses looked more or less like Mrs. B.'s.

Behind Alma, Clint Black sang, Silvita cried, Eddie and Tino laughed. In front of her, the big cat washed itself and a mockingbird sang in the mimosa tree.

Once when Alma had chased a ball over this fence, Mrs. B. had seen her through the screen and waved at her. She didn't really know Mrs. B., but they said hello when they passed each other. On the day of the funeral, Mrs. B. had said how sorry she was that Abuela had died. She probably wouldn't mind if Alma went into her yard, just for a little bit.

And Alma wouldn't be hurting anything.

And it didn't matter what anybody did anymore, anyway.

Alma climbed the fence. The cat stopped washing to stare at her from underneath his raised leg. The noise from her own house faded as Alma walked deeper into the yard and sat on the grass, hugging her knees. The tags on the cat's flea collar hung, shivering, but not quite jingling. "Jovita's dead," Alma informed him. "And Abuela's dead, and Mr. B.'s dead, and someday I'll die and you'll die and what's the good of *anything*?"

The cat's tags struck against each other as he stood up.

"But you don't care, do you?" Alma's voice felt thick in her throat.

With surprising nimbleness for such a bulky animal, the cat hopped to the railing, pushed through the screen, landed on the porch, trotted toward the back door, pushed open a panel in the lower half, and vanished inside.

Alma couldn't make out the meaning of the noises from her house anymore, but she could still hear the radio and Eddie's and Tino's voices. The mockingbird's liquid singing dripped out of the tree.

She didn't want to hear anything but Jovita.

Mrs. B. taught music at the university. Alma would have bet money, if she had any, that she owned a tape deck. And it would be quiet inside her house. But it wasn't worth thinking about. She couldn't get through a cat door. And she wasn't the kind of person who broke into houses. Any more than Jovita was the kind of person who hung out with gangs.

Maybe she should go to her friend Maggie's house. She'd have to walk, because she didn't have bus fare. Last summer it had been only three blocks, but Maggie's mother had gotten a promotion and they'd moved into an owned house closer to the university, on a block where you never saw gang signs. Alma thought of the people she knew who lived close, but Belinda Muñoz had gone to visit cousins, and Marina Vasquez never shut up. She'd talk and talk and talk about Jovita dying, and the last thing Alma wanted was to listen to anyone talk about this impossible thing.

Funny about the screen. From here, you couldn't tell there'd been space for the cat to get in.

Alma walked over to the screened porch, climbed the steps, and leaned against the rail. There was no hole, but the screen had come loose from the wooden framework. Alma pushed her arm through to the elbow and felt along the door frame until she found the hook that held the screen door closed. It wasn't hard to push it loose. Not wanting Eddie and Tino to hear the door slam—not that it would mean anything to them, but she didn't want them to hear it—she opened the door slowly and closed it softly after her.

The porch, scattered with cat toys, was the same size as her own. Mrs. B. kept her washer and dryer out here, well back under the roof, also a couple of chairs and some chewed-looking potted plants. The medium-sized cat, the yellow tiger, sprawled on the larger chair, looking at her upside down. He was friendlier than the others and sometimes came to rub against her when she sat on the back steps, watching Silvita in her play-pen. He had a hiccuping meow and an uneven purr. The round blue tag around his neck said he was Buddy and gave Mrs. B.'s name, address, and phone number. "Hey, Buddy," Alma said, reaching out her hand for him to sniff. "Jovita's dead."

"Muh-muh-muhouw," said Buddy, rubbing his ears against her hand. Alma laid her head down on the cushion beside him and let the tears fill up her eyes again, but she didn't really cry, just leaked a little. She sang *"La florita"* very softly. Buddy licked her cheek, but when she reached up her hand to pet him, he hopped down and strolled to the door. She sat glumly watching his straight-in-the-air tail bob away from her, but he didn't go through the cat flap. Instead he stood on his hind legs and stretched, pawing at the doorknob.

Alma watched him. The doorknob was about the height doorknobs usually are, with a second lock underneath, which was weird, but in old houses you get weird arrangements sometimes. And the cat door was big enough for a small dog, because the biggest cat was so huge. But she wouldn't be able to reach through and open the door from inside. She didn't think.

"Mu-mu-ow," stammered Buddy, and went inside. As if he was welcoming her.

If it was possible to break into Mrs. B.'s house using her cat door, she ought to know. Alma could test it, and if it *was* possible, she'd tell her about it.

Alma pushed open the flap with her hands. Beyond, she could see a red tile floor and the bottoms of cupboards. Tags jingled, out of sight. She lay on her stomach and pushed her arm through. The edge of the door cut into her shoulder, and all she felt above her was door. But what if she stuck her head through? Would her head even fit?

It did.

A ceiling fan turned slowly, and she could see the doorknob, with the dead bolt underneath it. Bracing her other arm against the porch, Alma strained upward and gripped the knob of the dead bolt. Righty tighty, lefty loosy was the rule, according to Lalo. It worked for screws, so why not with locks? She turned the knob to the left, almost lost her grip on it, and heard it click back into the door. The doorknob itself was harder. Her supporting hand was beginning to hurt when she felt the door give around her.

Alma let go and pulled her head out of the cat flap.

The door opened itself before her, invitingly.

- 5 -

the house

This kitchen was more or less like Alma's own, but with a tile floor instead of uneven linoleum, yellow rose wallpaper instead of bare white Sheetrock, and curtains instead of venetian blinds. The stove had a microwave, the cupboards were oak, and though the cats ate in here, Mrs. B. didn't, because she had no table. The only noise was the slow turning of the ceiling fan, the chime of the cat's tags against his bowl, and the crunching of cat food as the big cat ate. Buddy had vanished.

It was wrong to be in here.

So what?

"Meow," said the big cat accusingly.

"You shut up," said Alma. "You're the one who showed me how to get into the porch."

She went toward the door that would have led to the living room if this had been her own, smaller house. The big cat dashed out the other door, into a hallway.

Buddy stood in the middle of a mess of sheet music, books, and junk mail on a dining table, sniffing pink roses in a bud vase in the center. Alma barely noticed the bookcases and paneled walls of the dining room. A speaker was mounted on either side of an archway leading into the living room. Through the arch, she saw the front windows, blinds drawn against the afternoon sun, polished upright piano, shabby couch, and built-in shelves holding a guitar case and a sound system.

Not a stereo; a sound *system*. A CD player, two turntables, dual cassette deck, equalizer—the works! The couch was clawed up, faded, and covered with cat hair, the coffee table was invisible under dusty magazines, but the piano, the guitar case, and all the components of the sound system were as clean as if kept under glass.

This wasn't a living room—it was a listening room! On the tallest shelves stood LPs. Forty-fives perched in wire racks on top of CD cabinets and tiers of cassette bins. Medium-sized shelves held records midway between LP and forty-five—what on earth could you play *those* on? Names leaped randomly at her eyes as she approached the tape deck. John Lennon—Bessie Smith—Glenn Miller—Lynyrd Skynyrd—she didn't care about any of them. Only one voice was worth hearing today.

Power button. Eject button. Tape out of her pocket, into the deck. Play button. The music sprang up around her, rich and full, from four speakers—the two in the dining room and two more mounted beneath the ceiling above the sound system. Alma sank onto the hardwood floor, eyes closed, listening. Accordion, *bajo sexto,* guitar—rhythm, melody, harmony—Jovita's living voice backed by the band—singing about the moon floating above her when she took her pillow to the porch to sleep on a hot August night.

About the girl who danced with the devil at a cantina.

About a girl's *quinceañera.*

Rosalia'd had a small *quinceañera* shortly before Silvita happened, with a white dress and a mass and a party. Alma wondered if they'd be able to afford one when *she* turned fifteen.

A couple of times she heard a car drive by, but

when she peered through the blind, it was never Mrs. B.'s. She never got home till after Lalo did, Alma didn't think.

After Alma flipped the tape, she played around with the graphic equalizer, bringing up the bass, toning it down, testing the sound balance from the speakers, coaxing the melody of the big dance number out from behind the rhythm track. At last everything snapped into place—perfection—sound that held her inside it like air, that she felt with her body as well as heard with her ears. She sank back down and listened to the whole tape through again, both sides, forgetting to listen for cars. Forgetting she didn't belong here.

Alma wished she could turn into music or that it could continue forever, but the final chord faded and the hiss of the empty tape beyond the last song stopped with a click. The big cat walked up to within a few feet of her and watched her with cool, judgmental eyes. His name tag hung straight atop the silver rabies tag on his chest. Bopper. What a dumb name.

"What are you staring at?" asked Alma, rising to pop open the deck. Her stomach growled.

"Mew," said Bopper.

She looked around for a clock and found one on the

VCR tucked underneath the dusty TV. Four twenty-five. *Ay!* She needed to get home, and she needed to disguise where she'd been. She knew she hadn't hurt anything, but Lalo and Mama would only care that she'd broken in. She took out her tape, turned the power off, and scanned the rooms as she walked through them. She didn't seem to have disturbed anything, unless you counted the smallest cat, who skittered out of the kitchen as she came in. There was no way the cats could tell on her, and as far as she remembered, she hadn't touched anything but the sound system and the floor.

On the refrigerator, right above the ice maker, a sheet of paper fluttered, marked up with pink highlighter. *School of Fine Arts—Summer I.* All the courses highlighted were music classes, with *Burkhalter* under the *Instructor* column. Mrs. B. was teaching three classes, five days a week, the first starting at nine in the morning, the last ending at four-thirty in the afternoon. She'd be home soon.

Alma stuck herself back through the cat flap to rebolt the door once she was through. Turning the knobs right to lock them was harder than turning them left to unlock them had been, but by putting a crease in her neck and armpit straining against the hinge, she managed.

On the porch, she didn't stand up until she had peered between the screened-in railings at her own house. Mama's and Lalo's cars were in the drive, but no one was visible, and she couldn't hear anything, though she smelled chicken. Her stomach growled again. Relatching the screen door was as easy as unlatching it had been, and Alma climbed the fence slowly, with the least possible noise. To make doubly sure that no one suspected where she had been, she went around to the front of the house and ran up the porch steps noisily.

Inside, Mama looked up from watching a game show. She wore the flowered housedress that was her relief from uniforms—the hotel maid's uniform of her day job and the coveralls from her dishwashing job at night. Watching the afternoon game show while somebody else cooked her an early dinner was her big chance to relax for the day. "Where've you been?" she snapped.

"Jovita's dead," said Alma.

"That's not an answer!"

Rosalia ran out of the kitchen, Lalo following more

quietly. "What the *heck* did you think you were doing? Going off and leaving me with Silvita on my hands all day long! And Eddie and Tino—"

"I look after Silvita all day every day!" Alma flared up. "And all night, too! You can do it for once! You're her mother!"

Mama got up. "Don't yell at your sister."

"She yelled at me first!"

"She was worried about you. And don't yell at me, either. I can get that at work if I want it."

She wasn't worried about me one bit, thought Alma, mouth closed tight.

"So where did you go?" asked Mama again, with tired patience.

"Out."

"Don't talk like your brother. We called Maggie and Marina. They didn't know where you were."

"I was just *out.*" Suddenly Alma was weak in the knees, wanting to cry again. "Who cares? What difference does it make? Jovita's *dead.*"

"So what? People die every day." Mama's voice shook a little. "That's no reason to run off and not say where you're going."

"*Ay,* Mama, don't be so hard on her," said Lalo. "You

know she thought that singer hung the moon in the sky. She's back, and she's okay, and she won't do it again." He looked directly at Alma. "Will she?"

"No," said Alma.

And she meant it, when she said it.

- 6 -

the Silence

Silvita woke Alma up crying the next morning. Wondering groggily how long it would take for Rosalia to respond if she ignored it, Alma decided that finding out wasn't worth letting that relentless noise drill away at her ears. She changed Silvita. After that there was no point in going back to bed. She heard movement and voices in the kitchen, the slam of a car door, and the grind of an engine as Mama left.

Eddie and Tino slept in the living room. In the kitchen, Rosalia spooned potato and egg into a flour tortilla, and Lalo looked up from the funnies. "Feeling better?" he asked.

"Why should I?"

"Stop it," said Rosalia. "You're not turning mean

like Eddie, are you?" She held out her arms, and Alma traded Silvita for the package of tortillas.

"Sorry," mumbled Alma as she scooped egg and chorizo into a tortilla. "Have y'all seen my tape player?"

"Eddie took it when he ran off yesterday afternoon," said Rosalia. "Listen to the radio."

The radio was back to normal. The morning newsman didn't have any more to say about Jovita's death than last evening's TV news had. Less, actually. The TV news had interviewed crying neighbors. "I knew the gangs were here, but I never thought they'd kill our Jovita," a grown-up lady in a housecoat had said. "It must've been an accident," declared a wet-faced teenage girl, "like the old lady and the little boy. They were drunk or something. And it was dark." One boy with his hat on backward, gang style, said it wouldn't have happened if girls wouldn't be in gangs, as if drive bys were perfectly safe as long as guys did them. According to the DJ this morning, the police still had no clues about which gang had done it, and then he talked about something boring in South America.

"They'll never find out who did it," said Alma, picking at her breakfast. "Everybody's too scared of the gangs to tell."

"You don't know that," said Lalo. "Maybe somebody already told the cops something, and they're keeping it quiet so the gang won't come after the witness."

"*Claro!* You go on TV telling the whole world you saw who killed Jovita, you got a reason to be scared," said Rosalia.

Lalo left for school. Rosalia finished feeding Silvita and put her in the playpen with her stuffed dog while she looked at the want ads. Alma searched the living room and the closet, where Eddie kept his stuff since Lalo and Rosalia had moved into his old room, without finding her tape player. Rosalia turned off the radio in the kitchen and dialed the phone. Alma stood by the couch, poking Eddie till he blinked at her.

"Where's my tape player?"

"S'not yours," mumbled Eddie. "Get out of my face."

"It is, too, and you know it! Where is it?"

"Hocked it." Eddie shoved her away and rolled over.

"You *what!*" squawked Alma.

"Hush up!" Rosalia called. "I won't get any interviews if they hear kids fighting."

"How could you hock my tape player?" demanded Alma.

"It wasn't yours. Go away. I don't feel good."

"What did you do with the money?"

"Spent it. What do you think money's for?"

Alma wanted to pound her fists on Eddie's head, roll him off the couch, and stamp on him, hurt him all over, but she knew she couldn't, not even if he hadn't been bigger than her.

Instead she ran out onto the front porch, banging the door behind her, and hurled herself against the rail. *Ay!* She bent nearly double as her upper body tried to keep going after the railing stopped her. "I hate Eddie!" she muttered to the morning glories twining the rail. *"Lo odio, lo odio!"*

Saying it didn't make her feel any better. She hung over the railing, staring at the uneven grass below. They were getting an ants' nest beside the steps.

"Well, baby, you gonna stay in or go out? Make up your mind."

Mrs. B.'s voice was clear, but no louder than a radio turned down for night listening. Alma looked over to see her holding the door open, Bopper hesitating between her feet. She stepped out and pulled the door almost closed behind her. When it was no more wide open than the breadth of his head, the cat darted out, dashed halfway across her porch, and abruptly sat down to wash his belly fur. Mrs. B. laughed and closed the door.

I should tell her, thought Alma. *I don't have to say I went in, just that I know I could have.*

Mrs. B. wore a striped blouse, sandals, and makeup. Her gray-and-blond hair was braided back from her face, and gold earrings shaped like treble clefs dangled from her ears. She turned from bolting the door, saw Alma, and waved. Alma waved back.

"Good morning!" called Mrs. B., walking toward her car. "Having a good summer?"

"Jovita's dead," said Alma.

Mrs. B. stopped at her gate. "I heard about that. That singer. I was embarrassed I didn't know who she was. A local music celebrity—I should have known."

"She didn't sing Anglo kind of music," said Alma, letting her off the hook, careful to say the whole sentence in English.

"Music doesn't belong to any one group of people," said Mrs. B. "And it doesn't die, thank goodness!" She opened her car. "Don't be any more miserable than you can help. What happened is terrible, but you can still listen to her. Bye."

Last year's acorns popped and crunched under her tires as she drove away. Alma swallowed, and swallowed again. That was a funny thing to say. Almost as if she understood. But how could she?

And what difference would it make if she did?

Alma couldn't play her tapes. She couldn't go over to anybody else's house, because she had to baby-sit while Rosalia went job hunting. She couldn't play Abuela's old records because the turntable had broken months ago.

She turned up the TV loud so Tino and Eddie couldn't sleep. They shuffled off to the kitchen to scarf some cold pizza—there was always cold pizza in the fridge since Lalo became a delivery driver—and then left. She watched cartoons; played with Silvita; called Maggie, who wasn't home; called Marina and hung up after one ring; tried to read one of Lalo's science fiction books; played with Silvita some more; listened to the radio; and did the breakfast dishes. No matter how much noise she piled on top of it, the silence of death crouched in her ears. She fed Silvita and choked down a tortilla filled with miscellaneous leftovers, too full of silence to want food.

Lalo came home happy around three. "Hey, little sister," he said. "I deserve a beer. I got a hundred on my test today."

"That's good," said Alma, "but Eddie and Tino drank your beer."

Lalo frowned. "Where are they?"

Alma shrugged. "I don't know. I don't care, either. They hocked my tape player and spent all the money."

Lalo got himself a tamarind soda. "Where's Rosalia?"

"Job hunting."

"So it's just you and Silvita again?"

Alma nodded. "I wish—I wish Abuela was alive. She never got to see Silvita sit up, or roll over, or crawl." And if she were still here, the silence wouldn't be nearly so loud.

Lalo took the baby from her. "Here. You run off and play a while. I bet I can handle Silvita for an hour or so." All the same, he looked at her doubtfully as she wiggled in his grasp. "And I'll see about getting your tape player back. Okay?"

"Okay," said Alma, but she knew her player was long gone. The only thing she really wanted to do was go back to Mrs. B.'s house and listen to the other two albums on that marvelous sound system, and she couldn't.

- 7 -

the funeral

Eddie came home, without Tino but with a black eye, during Mama's game show. "What happened?" she demanded.

"*Nada,*" he said.

"Pretty painful-looking nothing," said Lalo. "C'mon, I'll put some ice on it."

Alma started to follow them into the kitchen, but Mama shook her head. Alma sat back down. "Why does Eddie have to be like that?" she asked.

"Like what?" asked Mama.

"Taking my tape player. Drinking Lalo's beer. Fighting. Like that. He didn't used to be."

"Oh, he always picked on you pretty good. Remember the Halloween he put peeled grapes and spaghetti in his treat bag and convinced you he got eyeballs and guts? And how he sang songs and changed the words so they meant something different?" Mama smiled unexpectedly and sang: "'God bless a chili dog, food that I love!' He'd sing that when you had to practice 'God Bless America' for the school show and mess you up, and you'd yell and yell."

Alma laughed without wanting to and made herself frown again. "That was for funny. Now he's just mean."

Mama shrugged. "Boys are like that."

"Lalo's not."

"Lalo's a man. Let Lalo handle Eddie. It takes a man to handle a boy."

Abuela handled him, and she wasn't a man, Alma thought, but she didn't say anything. She rolled a ball for Silvita to crawl after, straining her ears to hear the conversation in the kitchen through the applause and ringing bells of the game show. Lalo's voice was deep like the bass line of a song, Eddie's high and uneven, like static. They got gradually louder and louder until Eddie shouted: "Hey, at least I'm legal, man!"

Which wasn't fair. Even if Lalo's family hadn't gotten the amnesty years ago, marrying Rosalia would have made him a citizen. Alma couldn't hear his reply, but she heard Eddie interrupt: "You think just 'cause you marry my sister and take over my room you can run my life! Well, you can't! You're not such big stuff! And you can't make me do anything!"

The back door banged. A commercial came on. Mama fidgeted, but all she said was: "I wonder what's taking Rosalia so long."

"Job hunting takes a while when you're on the bus," said Alma. "Want me to start dinner?"

Lalo came out of the kitchen. "Sorry, Alma," he said. "He wouldn't even tell me where he hocked your player."

"I didn't think he would," said Alma. "Did he have a fight with Tino?"

"He wouldn't tell me that, either," said Lalo. "Maybe he'll talk to you, Mama?"

Mama shook her head and sank deeper into her chair. "I can't control that boy. He's like his father. Has to learn things the hard way, and even then he doesn't always learn them. When Manuel started acting like this, Abuela told him to join the marines, and it shaped him up, but they don't take fourteen-year-olds in the service."

"What about your brother?" asked Lalo, sitting down on the couch with Silvita between his feet. "Could you send Eddie to Laredo for a visit?"

"He'd hate that!" Alma said. Tío Manuel's kids never had any chance to get into trouble.

Mama rubbed her eyes. "My head hurts."

Footsteps trudged on the porch, and Rosalia came in, shoulders drooping, arms full of carryout from the fish fry near the bus stop. "It's too hot to job hunt and too hot to cook!" she said. "I'll need pocket money for tomorrow. All I have left after this is a quarter." She looked at Lalo and sighed. "*Ay!* Don't let her chew your shoelaces, *idiota!*"

Guiltily he pulled his feet away from Silvita.

So they ate, and Lalo and Mama went to their different jobs, and no one talked about Eddie anymore.

The next couple of days passed in a haze of heat and routine chores. Alma baby-sat Silvita while Rosalia made the rounds of fast-food joints and retail stores.

News about the Jovita investigation trickled in through the radio, the TV, and newspapers. She'd been hit three times by .30-30 rifle bullets, which matched a rifle found broken up, wiped clean, and discarded in the yard of a deserted house, where neighbors said drug deals often went down. Someone described the car used as a dark four-door with one light-colored door on the front passenger side. The company that made Jovita's records offered a reward for information and announced that it would release a special tribute album, all proceeds to go to the community center in Jovita's neighborhood.

The night before the funeral, Jovita's mother went on TV for the first time. "People are sending us so many flowers, we can't keep them all," she said. "I'm having them delivered to the hospitals. I know that Jovita is watching us and feeling good that so many people loved her so much. But if you really want to make her happy, take that flower money and send it to the community center, or the drug program, or the schools. Jovita is—" She stopped, and for a minute Alma wasn't sure she would go on. "Jovita was my precious girl, but she's not the only precious child to get hurt by the gangs. It's too late to help her now, but if you want to help her memory, do something to keep any more of our children from getting hurt."

Alma cried.

Eddie sneered. "Who does she think she is, preaching at people? Her precious girl was in the gangs herself, the old bag! Why doesn't she tell people that?"

Rosalia used up all the good job leads in two days and stayed home the day of the funeral, but she wouldn't take Alma, and she wouldn't let her go by herself. "We don't have a car," she said.

"We don't need a car," protested Alma, who had dug a black shirt and black jeans out of her dresser for the occasion. "There's special buses."

"I'm not carrying Silvita around in a howling mob in this heat," said Rosalia. "And I'm not letting you go, either! You could get trampled to death. And what if the gangs show up?"

"They wouldn't dare," said Alma.

"Oh, they would," said Eddie. "They're all going. Las Howling Madres, Los Chupacabras, everybody. If one stays away, the cops will think they did it."

So Alma watched the funeral on TV, but Eddie wouldn't shut up. When Rosalia tried to make him, he called her names until she took Silvita into her and Lalo's room and shut the door. "Look at all those idiots," he said as the camera panned down the long line of cars following the hearse: old junkers and new shiny vans, low riders and pickups, decorated with flowers and pictures of Jovita, honking their horns. The special buses lumbered at the end of the procession, crammed full of people dressed in black. Many were younger than Alma; quite a few women carried babies.

"They're all going to faint, standing around in black like that in this weather," said Eddie. "See, what did I tell you? That's the Chupacabras-mobile, that low rider there."

"They got a lot of nerve showing up," said Alma, glaring at the screen even after the car full of boys in gang colors was gone.

"Yeah, well, it takes nerve to be in a gang," said Eddie. "When I join, I'm going to be a Chupacabras."

Alma felt sick to her stomach. "You're not going to join."

"Oh, no? Who's going to stop me?"

The newscaster recapped Jovita's career, and her band, all in black, played bits and pieces of her songs, mostly the sad ones. Eddie sang along, changing the word, so that "Not Anymore" was about a dirty, lazy girl who dated too many boys. "Shut up!" Alma shouted at him, but he sang louder and louder.

Then the TV showed Jovita's mother and sister with the priest. "*Ay de mi!* He's going to start praying and preaching, isn't he?" Eddie groaned. "Time to change this channel!"

"Don't you dare!" Alma balled her fists and stood between him and the screen.

"Oh, yeah, you scare me something awful," said Eddie, shoving her aside and flipping the dial.

"Stop it! Stop it! Stop it!" Alma tried to shove him back, but he flipped the dial with one hand and fended her off with the other, laughing, as a music video, a war movie, an old sitcom, and a cartoon went by. "Why do you do this?" she shouted.

"I'll do what I want," he said. "I don't have to answer to you. Or Rosalia. Or your puke-perfect Lalo, either!"

Alma ran out the front door and down the street a couple of blocks, till lack of breath and the sweat running into her eyes stopped her. She leaned against a tree till she finished panting, then walked slowly around the corner to the alley. It was shadier back here, the untended grass slapping at her legs. The dogs at the house on the other side of the block barked at her, but she knew they wouldn't hurt her if she didn't go into their yard, and she had no plans to do that. She had no plans to do anything, but when walking toward home she came to Mrs. B.'s back fence, she stopped. The gate beside the platform where Mrs. B. left her garbage cans on trash days was open, and Buddy hunted in the long grass.

"Hey, Buddy," Alma said. "What you got?"

She watched him stalk, pounce, rustle around in the grass, then walk away, as if he'd never meant to catch anything anyway. She crouched and reached out her hand. He bumped his head against it, tags jingling. "I'm missing Jovita's funeral," she said, scratching his ears.

"Mr-ruh-rp," said Buddy, pushing his head farther into her hand. She rubbed his nose, then petted him from head to tail. The sun beat down on her black clothes, and sweat tickled against her ribs. Eddie was right about one thing—it was way too hot for black clothes.

Alma went through the gate. Maybe Mrs. B. had mended the screen.

She hadn't.

Maybe she'd locked the cat flap.

She hadn't.

Maybe she'd left the blinds open, so the living room would be visible from the street.

She hadn't.

Alma found the channel with the funeral just as the children from the music class at the community center joined hands to make the living rosary.

- 8 -

the music

After the funeral, Alma lay on the floor, letting the TV
run. It had been a good funeral—much better than her
grandmother's. Abuela had died shortly after Lalo got
his GED and started technical school, when there was
no money in the house at all. Mama's big brother, Tío
Manuel, had paid for part of it, but he and Mama had
argued about the best ways to do things. They'd all said
rosaries for her every night for a week, but there'd been
no living rosary, no eulogies, and Alma hadn't been
allowed to play the music Abuela herself had picked
out. Instead an organist from the church played music
that made Alma feel heavy inside. The priest had talked
about Abuela being blessed and free of pain in heaven.

Alma hadn't been back to church since then.

She tried to imagine Jovita and Abuela meeting in heaven, Jovita singing *"La florita"* for her and Abuela dancing a prizewinning dance, with heavenly choirs for backup. Some of the musicians who had made the old records Abuela treasured would be dead, too. Maybe they could jam, have *un gran baile* on a gold-paved patio behind the Pearly Gates, singing about the flowers coming back year after year. But she couldn't picture it. All she saw in her head was the gang members, to which the cameras at the funeral had returned time and time again—Las Howling Madres, in black, carrying roses red as blood; Las Princesas, holding instead of wearing their color caps with the appliquéd crowns. Everyone else at the funeral bowed their heads and cried freely. The gangs stared back at the cameras with blank eyes and stone faces. Then the camera pulled back, and newscasters started talking as the long black car with Jovita's mother in it pulled out of the cemetery.

Alma began to get the creepy feeling that she was being watched.

Looking up, she saw the smallest cat standing in the doorway to the hall. Alma lay still, meeting his alert yellow gaze. Holding his shoulders and hips tensely, he came into the room, circling to leave lots of space between them on his way to the couch. His tags jingled nervously, and he never took his eyes off her, even when he stopped at the couch and stretched himself to reach the top of the arm and dig in his claws. A soft popping sound stuttered across the TV voices as he worked his claws in and out of the fabric. Buddy, Bopper, Mrs. B. What was this one named? Bomber? Boy? Bugger? Bubba?

The sound of gunshots made them both jump. On the TV, a *novela* had picked up in the middle, and a villainous drug dealer had walked into a police ambush. Alma slapped off the power. "Sorry about that, cat," she muttered.

The cat crouched, a ridge of fur standing straight up along his spine, on the back of the couch. "*Es bien,* s'okay," Alma said, as if he were Silvita. "No guns here. It's safe here."

Safe. Not just from guns. From gangs. From a brother who didn't act like her brother anymore, from Silvita crying and Rosalia's moods changing every five minutes. From the empty places where Abuela should be. She couldn't go back yet. No way.

If she'd planned this, she could have brought over some tapes and listened to them.

She ought to change the channel back. What had it been on when she came in? She couldn't remember, but Mrs. B. certainly didn't watch the Spanish stations as a regular thing. She remembered what had been on the screen when she first turned on the power and looked in the *TV Guide* until she found something that might be it. Occasionally she snuck sideways looks at the cat. "Bubba?" she called experimentally.

The cat licked his paw and scrubbed it hard over his face.

If she left now, she'd have to walk around the neighborhood if she wasn't going home. She needed to go to the bathroom before she did that. Nobody could blame her for that.

Because the living room took up the whole front part of the house, the hallway was shorter than the one at home. It had paneling halfway up and blue-and-gold paper above that, hung with blown-up photographs, mostly of Mr. and Mrs. B.—in wedding outfits, in front of a statue of a man with a guitar, holding hands on the porch of this house before the trim was painted green. In one, a teenage girl with a blond helmet of hair and a sparkly dress played a grand piano. In another, a young man with a shaggy haircut played guitar on a high stool.

The bathroom was at the very end of the hall and was the same as the bathroom at home, only different, with green tile instead of blue, a cat box between the sink and the clothes hamper, and the shower curtain neatly drawn. Alma used the barest minimum of toilet paper and soap and waited to see whether, like the one at home, Mrs. B.'s commode needed its handle jiggled. It didn't.

Mrs. B. only had two bedrooms, not three, and they both had their doors open, so Alma could hardly help looking as she went back to the living room. The little one had a desk, lots of bookshelves, and a computer. In the other, Bopper was curled up like a big gray pillow in the middle of a yellow bedspread. Of course she shouldn't go in, but there was a music stand next to the dresser, and she found herself wondering what instrument Mrs. B. kept in her bedroom and if she played it every night before she went to sleep.

The house was too quiet. It was a house for music.

She couldn't listen to her own tapes, but Mrs. B. had more music than you could shake a stick at.

Alma powered the sound system and looked through the stack of six jewel cases next to the CD changer. Eric Clapton, Stevie Ray Vaughan, Carlos Santana—him she'd heard of. He did a concert at Sunken Garden Theater every year, though he was kind of old and didn't play *conjunto* or *tejano*. Patsy Cline. The Supremes. Melissa Etheridge. Oh, well. She could hear what they sounded like while she poked around and saw what else was here. She hit random play and Santana's "Black Magic Woman" spilled out of the speakers.

The cat watched her from the couch as she explored the CD racks. Except for hugely famous people like the Beatles and Elvis Presley, Alma couldn't tell from the names what kind of music any given CD was, but by looking at covers, she saw that one section was devoted to hard rock, another to country, another to classical, and so on. On the CD player, Santana was followed by a country song that almost made her cry, followed by a reggae song about shooting a sheriff, followed by a girl group with a rhythm track that made her swing her hips and hair as she moved from one CD rack to another.

One whole rack was full of bands, Glenn Miller and Tommy Dorsey and—when she had given up hope—*El conjunto Bernal* and *Santiago Jiménez y sus conjuntos*. Old-fashioned stuff, but she had often heard Abuela play these groups on scratchy old records. She hadn't known you could get them on CD. If Abuela were listening, she'd surely like to hear them.

Alma was on her way back to the CD player, walking through a blast of guitar work from a deep-voiced woman whose English she couldn't quite understand, when a couple of Spanish words leaped out at her from the midst of a crowd of early rock and roll. *"La bamba"*—that was on Jovita's second album! Alma plucked it out from between a double-CD collection of Buddy Holly (a geeky-looking guy with big glasses) and a single CD of the Big Bopper. The guy on the front didn't look Hispanic, and most of the song titles were in English, but there was *"La bamba"* and another Spanish title, *"Malagueña."* She'd try this Ritchie Valens person. Why not?

She was already at the CD player when the coincidence struck her. Bopper, Buddy, Ritchie. She punched the stop button, turned her head, and into the sudden quiet called: "Ritchie?"

The cat on the couch looked at her, moving his ears. "Is your name Ritchie?" she asked.

The ears twitched. He didn't come, but she'd gotten his attention.

So Mrs. B. named her cats after musicians. Cool.

Alma popped out the CD changer and set it carefully to one side, then loaded an empty one sitting next to the player. According to the VCR clock, she should have time to listen to all the tracks on all three discs if she didn't go home till after Lalo got back from school. That would still give her plenty of time to put the CDs back and leave before Mrs. B. drove up, as long as Mrs. B. didn't come home between classes. If she heard a car slow down and start crunching acorns, she'd hit the power, change the CDs, and dash. She practiced this a couple of times and was pretty sure she could make it out before Mrs. B. saw her.

But she hadn't told Rosalia where she was going. She didn't want a whole lot of questions when she got home. Using the playlists as a guide and trying to remember how Tío Manuel had done this on his CD player in Laredo last time they'd visited, she experimented until she succeeded in programming the tracks she most wanted to hear: the two Spanish ones from the Valens disc and a handful of Abuela's favorites from each of the others. That would leave her time to get home before everybody got too upset.

She didn't even notice the assumption in the back of her head—that she could come back and hear the rest anytime she wanted.

- 9 -

the song

Silvita fussed all night. She didn't need changing, and she kept spitting out her pacifier, so Alma carried her around and around, singing. She started off with lullabies but soon used up the ones she knew. She sang a couple of slow Jovita songs. Silvita seemed to like these, but as soon as Alma went to lay her back in the crib, she fussed again. So Alma walked her around some more, singing as much as she could remember of one of the hip-swinging girl-group songs on Mrs. B.'s CD and rocking Silvita in rhythm. Silvita gurgled, but Alma couldn't remember much except for the chorus. She started to improvise.

Abuela's gone.
Jovita's gone.
Just you and me now, baby love.
Rosalia won't come in this room.
Lalo's sleeping like a tomb.
Eddie's turned into a goon.
Mama gets up way too soon.
Baby, baby, baby!

Around the room she danced, Silvita's weight pulling at her arms. Matching pains rose in each bicep. No breeze came in the window. Sweat stuck her skin to the baby's. Silvita slobbered and smiled. Maybe now? Alma danced her over to the crib and lowered her toward the pillow, singing softly, begging her to sleep: *"Duérmete, por favor! Duérmete, por favor!"*

As soon as her head touched the pillow, Silvita's face crumpled, her feet kicked, her hands grabbed at Alma's dangling hair. With a sigh, Alma picked her up again.

Dancing in and out of the patch of grayish light on the floor beneath the window, swaying and dipping through the shadows in the corners, Alma sang in English and in Spanish. A salsa beat sneaked in. She sang about Jovita and Abuela never waking up again, about Mama cutting her sleep short to work, about Eddie staying out late in the dark and sleeping through the light of morning. Everyone slept, she sang, except the two of them, and didn't Silvita want to sleep, too?

Finally, finally, the baby's head sagged onto her shoulder, her eyes closed. Alma danced once more around the room to be sure, though her arms screamed for relief. Into the crib now, slowly, slowly, lowering her with a swinging motion. There!

Alma stood over the crib, shaking the soreness out of her muscles. Silvita rolled over, her wet cheek pressed into the flat pillow, her diapered bottom poking itself into the air. Alma backed away, feeling behind her with her feet so as not to step on any of the stray toys or shoes scattered on the floor. She reached her own bed and sat down, yawning with her whole body. When she squinted, watery eyed, at the clock, she saw that it was almost three in the morning.

Alma took her pillow down to the foot of the bed, which was more in line with the window than the head was, and stretched out. The tune, not quite the same as the recorded one anymore, continued to run in her head, trying itself out on guitar and accordion, *bajo sexto* and tenor sax.

It was too hot to sleep. Maybe that had been Silvita's problem.

Too hot to dance, too, especially lugging a big heavy baby. But she'd done it. Drat Rosalia, anyway.

Dancing around the floor with the baby while the whole world sleeps. A fragmentary music video flickered on Alma's closed eyelids, a big dance number, mothers and fathers and baby-sitters trying to dance their babies to sleep. In the middle of the stage, she danced with Silvita on her hip, both dressed in lacy white nightgowns. A whole band backed her up, vague in the shadows in the back of the set as she sang in a voice as full and rich as Jovita's: *"Duérmete, por favor! Duérmete, por favor!"*

The tune followed her in her sleep, mutating as it started and stopped and replayed, over and over. It still played softly in her head when sunlight on her face woke her. *Ay!* It was way too hot! She sat up groggily and stumbled across the room to pull the blind down. The crib was empty, and she heard the TV. The clock read ten-thirty. Ten-thirty on a Saturday. Mama would have left for her weekend job ages ago. Alma pulled on shorts and a tank top and padded barefoot down the hall to the bathroom.

"*Hola, dormilón,*" said Rosalia as she emerged a few minutes later. "If you think I'm making breakfast for you, you've got another think coming."

"I'm not a sleepyhead," Alma said. "I was up half the night taking care of *your* baby. Didn't you hear her fussing?"

"No," said Rosalia. "You should have knocked on the wall or something."

"Last time I did that, the only person I woke up was Lalo."

"I can't help it I'm a sound sleeper. What were you doing to wake her up, anyway?"

"*Nada!* She just woke up." Alma went to the kitchen, walking in rhythm to the tune in her head. By now it had no resemblance at all to the song she had started with, but it still swung at her hips. If she had an accordion, she could play it, she thought, pouring herself a bowl of cornflakes. Or even if she had a guitar or a piano, like Mrs. B., she could probably figure out how to play it. She tapped out the rhythm on the tabletop.

The cornflakes crunched in her ears. In the living room, Rosalia and Lalo argued, their voices rising and falling in competition with an infomercial. She couldn't tell what they were arguing about and didn't want to know. She wanted to shut the world off at her ears and listen only to the sounds in her head, but it didn't work.

Lalo came in and started rummaging around for leftovers for an early lunch so he could be at the store for his shift at noon. "Thanks for taking care of Silvita last night," he said. "It isn't really your job."

Alma shrugged. "Silvita doesn't care whose job she is." She chased a cornflake around the bowl with her spoon. "Do you think you'll ever have enough money to buy another accordion?"

"An accordion, that's kid stuff for me," said Lalo. "After I graduate and get a good job, then I'll have more important things to buy. We'll need to get our own place, and if Rosalia goes back to school, we'll need a baby-sitter."

"I could do that," said Alma. "I know how."

"I know," said Lalo. "But I don't graduate till December. You'll be in school when I get a job. Besides, wouldn't you like to do something with your life besides baby-sit?"

"Yeah," said Alma. "I'd like to play the accordion. Or the guitar. Or something. I don't think it's kid stuff."

"For you, maybe it's not. If that's what you want, we'll get you one. We'll find a way."

Alma drank the milk in the bottom of her bowl, thinking: *I already know a way.*

"You're a good kid," Lalo went on, sticking his plate of soft tacos into the toaster oven. "That's a tough thing to be. But you hang in there. Once I graduate and Rosalia and I can move out, it'll be a lot easier for you."

"No, it won't," said Alma. "You're the only one that sticks up to Eddie for me."

"Eddie won't need as much sticking up to after he gets his room back," said Lalo. "And if he finds a job, Mama can quit one of hers and be home once in a while. You'll see. Things'll get lots better next year."

Next year seemed awfully far away, and Alma wasn't convinced, anyway.

A friend of Lalo's picked him up so that Alma and Rosalia would have the car to get groceries. Getting groceries was a major undertaking. First they counted up their money and food stamps; then they made a list, deciding what needed to go on the stamps and what they needed to pay cash for; then they packed up Silvita and her diapers and juice bottle. Alma knew that the juice bottle would wind up on the floor at least three times. Silvita seemed to enjoy the sight of Alma chasing after it as it rolled between carts and stacks of canned goods. Then they had to make sure all the windows and doors were closed and locked.

"What if Eddie comes home while we're gone?" asked Alma. "He won't be able to get in."

"Don't bet on it." Rosalia sniffed.

As they pulled out, Alma looked longingly at Mrs. B.'s house. The car was parked in the street, the blinds were up, and Bopper lay on the sill of one of the open windows. Inside, Mrs. B. dusted her piano, moving to the beat of the music on her CD player. She didn't have her music up loud, but Alma could tell it was lively instrumental, with lots of brass and piano. Jazz, that was the word.

"Someday I'll have a big house and a sound system, and I'll know how to play all kinds of instruments," said Alma. "I'll teach music free at the community center, and—"

"Someday you'll have kids and a job and not enough money, just like the rest of us," interrupted Rosalia.

Alma shut her mouth tight and looked out the window, the hot wind of the moving car blowing her hair into her face, the soft pulse of her tune beating at her head uselessly. Trying to get out into the world, where it could be heard.

- 10 -

the guitar

The song nagged at Alma's brain all weekend and all
Monday and Tuesday while Rosalia looked for work.
She sang it over and over to herself and to Silvita, per-
fecting the lyrics, but she wanted an instrumental solo
between the second and third verses, and no sound she
could make with her voice satisfied her. Dragging up
from her memory everything elementary school music
classes had taught her about reading music, she tried to
write it down, but she couldn't be sure that the notes
on the page were right, that they would get up and
dance when played on a guitar.

She had decided on guitar by that time. Accord-
ions had more range, but she didn't know where to
find one.

Wednesday morning, at last, Rosalia got into shorts and a tank top instead of job-hunting clothes. Alma, planning ahead, loaded her book bag with a peanut-butter-and-banana sandwich, a can of cream soda, and her Jovita tapes.

"Where you going?" asked Rosalia, barely looking up from rolling plastic doughnuts at Silvita.

"Maggie's," answered Alma, picking the visit that would give her the best excuse to be away all day long. "I'm eating lunch with her."

"Okay," said Rosalia. "As long as you're back for supper. I'm making *arroz con pollo*."

Eddie moaned and rolled over. "Why do y'all have to make so much *noise?*"

Alma let the door slam behind her.

She turned as if going to the bus, walked around the block, and headed down the alley to Mrs. B.'s back gate. It didn't stand open this time, and Buddy wasn't there. She could hear Rosalia and Eddie fighting, with a background noise of TV, as she approached the porch. Mrs. B.'s other neighbor couldn't possibly see her through the screen of honeysuckle and mountain laurel along that fence. She unhooked the screen door.

Bopper was curled like a round throw pillow on the seat of the porch chair. "*Hola,* Bopper," said Alma, putting her hand down for him to sniff. "You know I won't hurt anything, *verdad*? You know it's okay."

He drew his nose back. Slowly she reached to scratch his ears, and he let her, even shoving his head up into her palm once. When he pulled his head away, she stuck hers through the cat flap.

Mrs. B. must have been running late this morning. She had left a coffee-stained mug and a plate of egg yolk, toast crumbs, and melon rind on the drain board of the sink. Alma hesitated before putting her cream soda into the refrigerator, where the milk was skim, the crispers were too full of fruit and vegetables, and the eggs were in the wrong sort of egg bin. The class schedule still hung crooked above the ice maker, suspended from a rainbow magnet. Nine to four-thirty. There was time to come home in the middle of the day—but Mrs. B. hadn't done that so far this week. Alma'd seen her get home every day at five. Alma hurried to the living room, suddenly afraid that the blinds would be up.

The living room was cool and dim. The guitar waited on its shelf.

The case was black, except where it was scratched or worn at the edges, where the frayed gray cardboard showed through. Alma set it carefully on the piano stool and flipped the latches. It was an acoustic guitar, not the electric one she had imagined playing in the video, but it had six strings, and that was the main thing. Putting the worn strap around her shoulder, she settled it in her hands, holding it the way musicians held guitars on TV. No doubt it would be easier when she was taller and had longer arms. Mama said she would get a growth spurt any time now. She strummed the strings with her fingers, but they were loose and made no sound to speak of.

"Tuning," she said. Musicians had to tune their instruments before playing them. But how did you do that? She played around with tightening the strings and got sounds out of them, but whether they were the right ones or not, she couldn't be sure. She tried to pick her song out on it, anyway, remembering that she needed to hold the strings down at the neck as well as plucking them above the sound board. But how was she supposed to know which string to hold when or where to hold it? She'd never turn her song into real music at this rate!

She kept trying until her fingers and arms were sore, and in the end she was no closer to the music in her head than she had been when she stuck her head through the cat flap. Tears of frustration blurred her vision as she lifted the strap from around her neck. All this waiting for nothing!

Well, not quite nothing. She dug her Jovita tapes out of her book bag and popped them into the cassette deck on Mrs. B.'s sound system.

But not even Jovita's soaring notes could take up all her attention today. Her own song chafed at her brain and made it impossible to sit still. She tried to approach Ritchie when she saw him stalking out of the bedroom, but he avoided her, slipping sideways into the kitchen and from there out the cat flap. The only sign of Buddy was yellow hair sticking to the couch cushions. She wandered round the living room, scanning the CD racks and shelves. Songbooks, textbooks, books about people she guessed were musicians, though in most cases she didn't know the names. Apart from a few potted cacti, the only ornaments had some music theme, and most were inscribed *To the World's Greatest Teacher* or something like that. She worked her way around to the shelves below the guitar case, avoiding the smiling gaze of Mr. and Mrs. B.'s picture on the piano.

The shelves below the guitar were tall enough to hold bundles of sheet music and extra-tall softbound books. *Introduction to Guitar: Teacher's Guide,* she read. *Teaching Music: Theory and Practice.* Handbooks, workbooks, music books, all dog-eared and split-spined.

It would probably be useless, but Alma pulled out *Introduction to Guitar. Anton Burkhalter* was written in black Magic Marker on the cover. So Mr. B. probably was also a music teacher. She hadn't known that. She didn't care much now, since he wasn't around to teach her. The question was, did the book say anything useful?

Jovita sang encouragingly as Alma flipped through it. Diagrams showed finger positions and named strings. The text gave tuning instructions. It advised tuning your instrument to match the notes on one you already knew was tuned.

Yes! Mrs. B. played this piano! She must keep it in tune. Alma went hunting for a book that would show her which note was which on the piano, found one, and turned Jovita off.

It wasn't easy. The same note could never sound quite the same on a piano as on a guitar. If it could, what would be the use of having both instruments? But she got them as close as she could, then sat down at the piano stool with the book open on the music stand and set to work.

Narrow sore spots grew into the tips of her fingers from holding down the strings and an ache into the muscles of her hand from holding the pick. She chewed her lip, playing through the scales until her hands began to know them, trying to pick out her song, failing, playing through the scales again. She gave up on her song and went for something simple: "Three Blind Mice," laid out in the book in musical form for her. Her stomach growled. Her shoulder hurt.

Buddy hopped onto the piano and walked across the lid to stand in front of the open book. "Get off of there!" Alma scolded, lifting him. He got his front paws back onto the piano by the time she had his back paws free. She picked him up and set him on the floor, but he hopped up and stood in front of the book before she got turned back around. She tried again, and he stuck his claws into the page. Her stomach growled again.

"Oh, all right," she said. "I'll take a lunch break. Keep your silly book."

Buddy looked at her with eyes that had no pupil, flipping his tail against the piano.

She restarted the tape and fetched her lunch from the refrigerator. Jovita's voice filled the air around her, and she felt good. The book wasn't the same as a human teacher, but she could do this. And when she had taught herself to play guitar, she would take her song out of her head and put it into everybody else's ears. She would be like Jovita, but she wouldn't waste time on drugs, or gangs, or drinking. She'd go straight to leading a band, singing at dances, making records and videos. And she would do worthwhile things with the money, just like Jovita.

She'd pay for Rosalia to have a baby-sitter and finish school. She'd pay off Lalo's student loan and buy him a car. She would take care of Mama so she could quit her jobs. And Eddie—Eddie—

Alma couldn't think of anything she would want to do for Eddie that he would like. She sure wasn't going to give him a bunch of fancy clothes and a flashy car, not after he stole her tape deck. Maybe it would be enough if he had his own room in the big house she would buy—no, that she would build! It would have an elaborate sound system, huge rooms, and a deck out back where she would host parties. All the best bands would come to her parties, and they would jam all night.

But first she had to teach herself the guitar, and she couldn't do that sitting here. She looked in the kitchen closet, carefully pulled a broom and dustpan out from behind a big plastic bin full of cat food, and when she was done sweeping up her sandwich crumbs put them back exactly where she had found them, though it took her three tries to get the broom balanced at the right angle. Back at the piano, she scratched Buddy's ears until he purred, then slid the book out from behind him.

"Sorry, Buddy," she said. "But I need this. It's going to make my fortune!"

- 11 -

the good time

Alma could no longer waste time going around the block to get next door. Rosalia might find a job any day, and then Alma would be stuck baby-sitting. Rosalia never asked any questions beyond: "Did you have a good time at Maggie's?" As long as she got home before Lalo and Mama and Maggie never called while Alma was supposed to be at her house, no one had any reason to ask questions. Any day Rosalia didn't spend job hunting, Alma could spend learning the guitar.

So she supported Rosalia's reasons for turning down, or not applying for, jobs Lalo thought she should get. She wouldn't take any job that required working nights because that would leave Alma alone with

Silvita too long. Fast-food places made her too dirty and sweaty. Delivering newspapers wasn't really a job, and telemarketing was just rude. "Why do you want me to take such nasty jobs, anyway?" she demanded one day during a fight.

"You dropped out of high school," snapped Lalo. "Dropouts only *get* nasty jobs."

"And whose fault is it I dropped out?" Rosalia started to cry. "It wasn't my idea to have a baby!"

"It wasn't my idea, either!" Lalo threw himself into a chair and stared at a book. Rosalia stood in the middle of the living room, crying. Eddie turned the TV up louder. Silvita, sitting up in the middle of her toys, looked as if she might cry, too, so Alma distracted her with a stuffed turtle. Lalo dropped the book, put his arm around Rosalia, and said: "Look, I'm sorry. I didn't mean that." They went to their room, but Eddie didn't turn the TV back down.

Eddie took the newspaper job, assembling and selling them outside the grocery store. Lalo offered to make him put aside some of his money to buy Alma a new tape deck, but Alma told him not to bother. "He wouldn't ever do it," she predicted, "and you'd just have to fight about it every week."

Besides, she thought but did not say, *no deck Eddie could buy with newspaper money would be half or a quarter as good as Mrs. B.'s.*

"You're a good kid," Lalo told her. He was always saying that.

"Not so very," said Alma. "There's just some things you can't do anything about."

"Now, don't you think like that!" Lalo stopped smiling. "You got to take your chances. You want it, you go get it."

So all through the rest of June, when the chance came to go to Mrs. B.'s, Alma took it, even on hot, lazy afternoons when she'd rather have gone to Maggie's house for real and lain around watching TV and sipping cold drinks.

First she followed, as well as she could with no teacher, one of the lessons in the guitar textbook until she was so tired and frustrated she couldn't go on or until she was sure she had it right.

Then she'd take a break, play with the cats, wander around the house looking at stuff. She didn't touch anything, or if she did, she always made sure she put it back exactly. Mostly Mrs. B. was pretty tidy, but sometimes Alma had to walk around a shoe in the middle of the floor, and there were certain items of furniture that never got dusted, so she was careful never to even bump into them.

The instrument in Mrs. B.'s bedroom was a recorder. Alma'd stayed late at school part of last year, taking recorder for extra credit, until the program that brought the teacher and instruments ran out of money. Alma was pretty sure she could still play "Three Blind Mice" on one, but she put her hands behind her back when she went near it. It was one thing to borrow someone's house and another thing to share germs!

There were posters on the bedroom walls, which was weird for a grown-up—posters for rock concerts and a ragged-edged one in a fancy frame for a movie starring the Beatles. The computer room had books in it, mostly thick ones in English that were too hard, and toward the end of June a couple of music magazines got left on the dining table for Alma to read bits from and replace carefully under the accumulating mail.

After her fingers felt normal again, Alma would work on her song, which stubbornly refused to retain the shiny, vague perfection of the song in her head. But the satisfaction of getting her hand, the guitar, and her ear all lined up so that one bar or another became real could wipe out days of frustration in a moment. Then at last, empty and tired, she would crank up the sound system.

Even Alma couldn't endlessly play the same three Jovita tapes over and over, so she started keeping her whole tape collection in her book bag. Emilio and La Mafia and Selena kept her happy for a couple of days. But there was no ignoring the CDs surrounding her. She poked around in Mrs. B.'s music. Curiosity led her to play the three musicians she thought of as "the cats." Mostly they were too old-fashioned, but a few tracks made her dance in spite of herself.

She sampled every female artist she found. Over and over she sang along, trying to soar like Marian Anderson, or rock like Melissa Etheridge, or pulse like Diana Ross. When she expanded her search to include groups, she found more women, mostly vocalists, buried among the men. She would not be buried, Alma resolved. She would *lead* her band!

By now the real cats were used to her. Bopper, when he felt like it, would bump his head against whatever part of her was handy until Alma petted him good and hard. When he didn't feel like it, she couldn't get near him, but that was okay. Buddy was hilarious to watch chasing after a catnip mouse or a jingle ball and amazing to see leap to the top of the refrigerator or a high shelf in a single bound. Alma kept watching for him to knock something over, but he never did. Only Ritchie galloped away whenever he saw her.

By then it would be almost four o'clock, and she would begin to get ready to leave. First, replace the guitar and all the guitar books, close the piano, make sure the piano stool was in the same position it had been in that morning. Then put all the CDs back where they came from and replace the original changer, being careful to turn the power off. Check the area where she'd eaten for crumbs, check the refrigerator for a forgotten soda or piece of fruit. Take a walk around the house, scanning for signs that she had passed through. Look through the kitchen and porch windows, make sure the coast was clear. Let herself out through the back door, reach back in through the cat door, bolt it. Out through the screen door, latch it.

Safe, and ready for the next day.

Things went well at home, too, during those days— about three weeks only, but they stretched to hold so much that Alma could never keep track, later, of how short the time had really been. Eddie vanished with

Tino for hours and even days at a time, and Alma couldn't worry about him the way everyone else did. As long as he wasn't around, he didn't pick on her and he didn't cause fights. Lalo and Rosalia sometimes fought, mostly when Rosalia wanted to go out and Lalo said they couldn't afford it. But Lalo made A's, and Silvita grew daily, crawling around the house as nimbly as Mrs. B.'s cats.

Rosalia ran after her, but when she was home, Mama sat back and laughed as Silvita scooted on all fours from room to room. "What're you worrying about?" she scoffed at Rosalia. "All the cabinets are babyproof, and we got those baby gates across the outside doors. She can't get into anything."

"Mama, how can you say that?" demanded Rosalia. "There's plenty of dangerous things in this house! Why, she could—"

Alma saw the disaster about to occur and lunged, too late, as Silvita grappled a wastebasket and sent it straight over. "Silvita, no!" she cried out, in chorus with Rosalia, as wadded Kleenex and plastic wrappers tumbled onto the carpet.

Mama leaned back in her chair and laughed some more.

Rosalia looked up from pulling a happily giggling Silvita out of the mess. "What if she tried to eat a plastic wrapper? She could choke herself!"

"That's what I used to think about you," said Mama, "but you never did."

"You didn't think it was funny when Alma used to make messes," said Rosalia. "You'd get so mad, I thought you'd bust!"

"And your *abuela* laughed," said Mama. "What goes around comes around. Someday Silvita'll be fussing at your grandchildren, and you'll be laughing."

Rosalia flushed. "I don't have to be like you!"

"The stick doesn't fall far from the tree." Mama shrugged, taking Silvita into her lap, and started a finger game. *"Este dedito compró un huevo; este dedito lo cocinó. . . ."*

Mama was still playing with Silvita and Rosalia was still muttering about this fifteen minutes later when she started dishing up supper. "I don't care what she says—I'm not like her! I won't be!"

"What's wrong with being like Mama?" asked Alma, setting the table.

"What's right with it?" demanded Rosalia in an angry whisper. "Look at the way she spoils Silvita! She never played with you after our father left. I remember. Even when she was home, she wasn't home!"

"She had all her jobs to go to, and you were too little to baby-sit," said Alma. "Abuela took care of me all right."

"If she'd been able to keep a man at home, she could have baby-sat us all herself!"

"Marina's and Belinda's fathers are at home, and their mothers have jobs. Most mothers have jobs."

"Oh, you don't understand!" Rosalia dealt out tortillas like cards. "My children aren't going to drop out of school and hang out with gangs. I'm going to love them!"

"Mama loves us!" protested Alma, feeling hollow.

"When you have kids, you'll understand."

"I'm not having kids," announced Alma. "I'm leading a band."

"*Sí, sí.* I was going to be a fashion designer."

Alma sort of wished they hadn't had this conversation, but by the next day, the Fourth of July, she had other things on her mind. Eddie disappeared somewhere. Lalo had no school and traded shifts with one of the other pizza drivers to get the evening off. Mama went to her daytime job but not to her evening one.

In the morning, Lalo drove Rosalia, Alma, and Silvita out to meet his family for a picnic on Canyon Lake. Lalo and Rosalia had tried living with his family first, but his mother and Rosalia hadn't been able to get along. Knowing this made Alma nervous, but they talked happily about Silvita's growing as they laid out the picnic, so that was all right. While the grown-ups claimed a table and an outdoor grill, Alma and Lalo's little sister ran down to the lake, jumping in and out of the water.

After all the hot dogs were eaten up and the grown-ups ran out of things to say, but not before Alma was tired of playing in the water, they drove back to town to pick up Mama. "Now aren't you glad we didn't go out those nights you wanted to?" Lalo asked Rosalia quietly, when his family drove on ahead. "If we had, we couldn't treat our mamas to dinner."

"Hmmm," said Rosalia.

They got into a steak house before the dinner rush started, so that when they left, there was still plenty of time to get a good spot for the fireworks. Silvita fell asleep during the long, dull wait for darkness, and the first bang woke her up crying, but Alma had a good time, anyway.

Coming home late, they had to maneuver between extra cars on the street. Mrs. B. was having a party. Alma went to bed with the half-unheard sound of Buddy Holly drifting against her ears, filled full of happiness.

There was no way to tell that the good times would end the next day.

- 12 -

the bad time

Silvita slept through the night, and Alma woke on her own, still feeling good, before Mama left for work. The heat made her skin feel slobbery with sweat everywhere anything touched it, so she put on shorts and a tank top and tried to make her hair into a bun on top of her head with a hair scrunch, the way Abuela used to wear hers in summer.

She heard Lalo showering and saw Eddie asleep on the couch on her way to the kitchen. Mama was eating scrambled eggs with salsa and Rosalia was making juice. Alma helped herself to eggs, too, and they talked about Silvita and fireworks. The radio played La Mafia's newest song.

Lalo came in, barefoot in jeans, as Mama gathered her stuff together for work and the news came on. "Police finally have a clue in Jovita's murder," said the DJ.

Alma froze in the act of kissing Mama good-bye.

"The gun found thrown away near the scene is definitely the one that killed her, and they've traced it to a pawnshop on South Zarzamora. The pawnshop owner is one of the businessmen who contributed to the reward for finding Jovita's killer, and he has already turned over all his records to the police."

Alma didn't know what her face did, but Mama said: "It may not get them anywhere, even if they find the person who bought it. They still have to prove who used it."

"They'll find out something," said Lalo. "Even if the owner lies. The cops know how to dig around lies for the truth."

"What good does finding out do?" asked Rosalia. "Jovita will stay dead."

"The person who killed her shouldn't get away with it!" said Alma. "He should be dead, too!"

"His gang'll go straight out and kill somebody else. You want to kill them all?"

"If it stops them!" Alma felt hot inside.

Mama patted her cheek. "Don't think about it. There's nothing you can do." She kissed the top of Alma's head, sending the bun tumbling down, and left.

The day was not as bright as it had been, though it was every bit as hot. The radio played *"La florita."* Lalo and Rosalia ate their scrambled eggs and drank their juice. Alma fixed her bun again, making a ponytail, twirling it into a tight circle, and wrapping the end around the scrunch.

Silvita woke up, so Alma took her out to Rosalia, who laid aside the classified ads to take her. Alma turned off the radio and sat on the floor in front of the TV, with the sound turned low so as not to wake Eddie, to watch a cartoon about a rock star who was also a superhero. He caught a pusher dealing drugs at his concerts and went after the drug ring. "My fans deserve better than to be preyed on by scum like you!" he said to the pusher. His music was too jangly, and, watching his fingering with a critical eye, Alma saw that the animator didn't know how to play the guitar. Eddie snored on the couch. Silvita giggled as Rosalia played *tortitas* with her, patting little hands together. Lalo went back to the bedroom to finish dressing and reappeared almost at once, holding his sneakers. *"Ay de mí! Mira!* I can't wear these!" He poked his fingers out the toe of one shoe, the rubber flapping loosely.

"Maybe we can glue the sole back on," suggested Rosalia.

"Naw, there's a hole in the other one. Where's my leather shoes?"

"What am I, your maid?"

"Silvita and I were playing train with them in the hall yesterday while y'all packed the car," called Alma.

"Thanks for putting my stuff back!" said Lalo, less sarcastically than he was entitled to. She heard him go down the hall. "Here's one." He looked behind the open bedroom door.

A cereal commercial came on. It was time for Lalo to leave, or he'd be late for school. Alma tried to remember where she and Silvita had been playing. "Eddie's closet was open," she said, going to the door in the middle of the hall. "Maybe it got kicked in there." She opened the door and bent down on her knees to root through Eddie's stuff on the floor—tennis shoes, a half-deflated football, his defunct boom box. She picked up a black nylon jacket that had fallen on top of a box and saw the shoe. As she picked it up, she saw inside the box, which contained old school notebooks, copies of *Mad* magazine, and a Ziploc bag full of white powder.

Alma's brain shut down. She knew what it was. She'd seen the cop shows, had paid attention at anti-drug assemblies, and not ten minutes ago had watched a cartoon version of this very thing. But she couldn't get past that to any sort of reaction. Her throat shut tight, so there wasn't room to force a word through.

Lalo came up behind her. "There it is!" he said cheerfully, bending over to take the shoe from her. "Thanks, Alma! I—"

His voice stopped as he saw it, too. But he didn't stop moving. He reached past Alma and lifted the bag out of the box, revealing Alfred E. Newman's sarcastic grin. "Do you know what this is?" he asked quietly. Too quietly.

Alma nodded.

"Do you know how it got there?"

Alma shook her head, though it was almost a lie. Her bun tumbled down into a mere ponytail.

Lalo backed out of the closet and stepped loudly down the hall to the living room, where the cartoon music jangled away in the rhythm of a chase scene.

"Eddie. Wake up!"

Alma's eyes locked with Alfred E. Newman's.

"Wake up!" roared Lalo. The house shook as something hit the floor. Silvita started to howl.

"Keep it down!" yelled Rosalia, stalking down the hall behind Alma.

"You see this? Look at this! What is it, Eddie?"

The cartoon character sang unintelligibly. Silvita cried.

"S'laundry detergent, man," mumbled Eddie. "Get it out of my face."

Rosalia gasped. Alfred E. Newman had no reaction.

"Right," sneered Lalo. A sharp, short sound, skin hitting skin, made Alma wince. "What's the matter with you, bringing coke into our house?"

"*Mi casa,*" Eddie spoke up. "It ain't yours. We just let you live here! What were you doing in my closet?"

"This is your mother's house!" Lalo was as loud as a train. "Where your baby niece lives, remember? Where your little sister lives, remember? Alma found this, Eddie. Your *hermanita* found your bag of hard drugs! Think about it!"

"You got no right to yell at me!" If Lalo was a train, Eddie was a tornado. "I don't have to take this from you!"

"Yes, you do! I ought to—"

"Shut up! Shut up! Shut up!"

Alma jumped back, losing eye contact with Alfred.

"Just because you got my sister pregnant that doesn't make you my boss! I'm so sick of you acting like you're better than me when all you ever did—"

Alma stood up.

"Don't you dare say that!" screamed Rosalia, prompting Silvita to scream even louder. "We ought to throw you out of this house! What if Silvita'd gotten into this stuff?"

Alma went through the kitchen.

"If everybody'd stay out of my closet, nobody'd get into anything! Don't I have any rights?"

Alma went across the yard, the ruckus less clear with distance but still audible. Mrs. B. was on her porch, locking her front door.

"Where'd you get it?" demanded Lalo. "From Tino?"

Mrs. B. turned her head toward Alma's house as she walked toward her car. Alma stood back in the shadow of a rose of Sharon, hoping Mrs. B.'s Spanglish wasn't good enough to understand what all the shouting was about.

"What do you think I am? A rat?"

"I think you're a *cholo* that doesn't care what happens to the rest of his family!"

Mrs. B. got into her car and drove away. Last year's acorns were all demolished now; the tires hardly crunched.

"Why should I care? Who cares about me? Nobody, that's who! Not one person in this whole house!"

Alma climbed the fence, ran across the yard, and fumbled at the screen door, letting it bang behind her. Everyone's shouts blended together now, a babble of random noise. She thrust her head and upper body through the cat door, and strained to turn the doorknob.

Inside, Mrs. B.'s house was cool and almost quiet, the noise from next door not much louder, beyond the closed windows, than the mumble of pigeons. Alma ran to the living room, where Bopper sprawled on the glossy piano, flew past him, landed on the couch, tucked her head down, and buried herself in the cushions.

- 13 -

the memory

Alma tried to practice the guitar, but she was all thumbs, and when she sang her song, it sounded sugary sweet and empty.

No one would ever want to listen to it. She would never own her own guitar, or accordion, or any other instrument and would never lead a band. Someday she would get pregnant and get married—or maybe she wouldn't even get married; some people didn't. She would have a dead-end job or maybe two, and her kids would grow up to join gangs and push dope and get pregnant, and what was it all for?

Mrs. B.'s CD changer was loaded with the discs she had played at last night's party. Alma turned the sound way down so it wouldn't be audible outside, flipped on the power, and hit random play. Elvis and Buddy Holly, Ritchie Valens and the Big Bopper and the Beatles, all sounded cheerful even when they sang about broken hearts. That was what music did: took bad feelings and made them feel good.

Alma would never be able to do that.

She would never feel good again.

Bopper let her pet him. "Eddie probably has to go to jail now," she said to him. "The only way out of it is to rat on the people he got the coke from. And if he did, they'd pull a drive by and we'd all get shot." There'd never been a drive by in this neighborhood, and it would be Eddie's fault if there was one now, but he probably wouldn't be home for it!

There'd been way more in that Ziploc than he could have bought with his newspaper money. Had he stolen it? Or was he hiding it for somebody? Or—

"Why should I care, anyway?" she asked Bopper. "He's only ever mean to me. I hate him!"

But she didn't want to hate him. She wanted her old brother back, the one who had rescued her from being beaten up, who had bought her a Jovita tape for her birthday, who had played board games and Barbie dolls with her when she was little. Awful things had happened to the dolls when he played, like an earthquake striking when Barbie and Ken went to a movie or aliens (represented by troll dolls) kidnapping Skipper, but none of her friends' brothers had ever played dolls with them at all.

What had happened to that brother?

She remembered the last time she had seen him. On a rainy autumn afternoon, he had come home from school late after band practice. Alma and Abuela had been in the living room, playing scratchy old dance records. Tony de la Rosa's accordion interrupted itself with a thrilling banshee screech as Alma glided around and around the room. "That's not how you dance!" Eddie had laughed, dropping his book bag and the rental sax by the couch.

"It's the best I can do by myself," Alma had retorted. "Abuela won't teach me."

"Abuela *can't* teach you." Abuela had defended herself, stretched on the couch with her leg up. "I've got arthritis in my hip something awful."

"Here," said Eddie, striding into the middle of the room and holding out his hands. And he had taught her to dance, *el tacauchito,* the smooth gliding dance that belonged to the music. He had made fun of the eagerness that had kept her perpetually half a beat ahead of the tune, but he had danced with her while Abuela counted time and Tony de la Rosa played the accordion from the ancient turntable in the corner.

After a bit Eddie had turned the turntable off and put a tape into his new boom box. "That's enough old stuff," he had said, and pushed down the button to let Jovita's voice come rolling out. Jovita—the big dance number from the first album—the *"Jovita polkita"*—he had taught her the moves and the strut and the laughing fling of the head that went with that music.

She had forgotten he had taught her that.

That was the night Rosalia brought Lalo home for dinner. They had both been quiet and distracted until Mama came home. Eddie and Alma had been chased off then to play backgammon in Eddie's room while the grown-ups talked, yelled some, and talked some more. She and Eddie had argued, and she had kicked over the board and run to the kitchen to eat the last of the *pan dulce* so Eddie couldn't have it. He had followed her and eaten *pan dulce* anyway. They had almost made up when the four grown-ups (but she saw now that Rosalia and Lalo hadn't really counted as grown-ups back then) came frowning into the kitchen, and Rosalia had announced: "Lalo and I are getting married."

Alma had clapped, scattering crumbs. Eddie had looked blank. "You're only a junior," he had said. "What are you getting married for?"

"It's not perfect," Lalo had said. "But it's the best thing we can do."

Then Eddie had dived into Lalo, shouting: "You got her pregnant, didn't you? You creep!"

Abuela had taken Alma away from the fight, and she didn't know how it had ended. Only now she thought that it never had ended.

Thinking about it here in Mrs. B.'s house, with Elvis rocking all around her and Bopper strolling into the kitchen and Ritchie washing his paws in the hallway, Alma could even make sense of Eddie's anger. Lalo and Rosalia shouldn't have started a baby by accident. Then when they'd tried to live in Lalo's parents' big house, Rosalia had fought with his mother all the time, and they'd had to come home where there wasn't really room. Mama rearranged the rooms so that Eddie was stuck sleeping on the couch, so that made him mad at her, too. To be fair, Alma couldn't see any other way to work it, but it *did* stink from Eddie's point of view.

And the doctor bills for having the baby had sucked up all the money that came into the house. Then Lalo got his GED and decided he needed to go to technical school, which meant quitting the construction job he'd had for a while. No more band practice for Eddie, because they couldn't afford to rent the sax. No more new tapes for anybody, only ones they copied from friends. Eddie hit his growth spurt, and Abuela had taken up Lalo's old pants to fit him, but he wouldn't wear them. He'd rather cut his old pants off at the knees and go to school looking like a Salvation Army reject.

Then Abuela had died, and Alma was still kind of mad about that herself, though she didn't know who she was mad at.

What Alma couldn't see was where Eddie got off being mad at *her*. She hadn't done a thing to him. Unless he thought there was something wrong with her liking Lalo when he didn't.

But Lalo had gotten his GED and enrolled in the technical school so he could get a good job while Eddie sat around being mad, hanging with Tino, and wanting to be a Chupacabras. Lalo and Rosalia had done something stupid, but they were trying to make up for it. Eddie was going right on being stupid, as far as Alma could tell.

And by having that coke he was stupiding himself straight to jail! Well, she wouldn't miss him! She wouldn't go visit him. She hoped he never got out! And someday—someday—

A noise, soft and harsh, fell into the silence between tracks on the CD player. Alma looked around as a new rhythm started. Between drumbeats, the sound choked and jingled.

Ritchie wasn't eyeing her suspiciously anymore. He jerked his upper body back and forth, half a beat off from the music, faster and faster. He didn't run away when Alma walked toward him, wondering if he was sick, and what she could do about it if he was. "Hey, Ritchie!" she called softly. "S'matter?"

"I'm gonna tell you how it's gonna be," sang Buddy Holly.

Ritchie's collar had come loose, and he had caught his lower jaw in it while washing his chest. He made choking, gasping sounds as he tried to jerk himself free, his tags jingling wildly. Alma made soothing baby talk noises and knelt beside him. "Hold still, baby," Alma crooned. "Poor Ritchie baby cat, hold still. I'll get you loose."

The moment she touched him he tried to leap backward, choking worse than ever. Alma lunged and caught him by the collar, terrified that he would break his own jaw as he fought her, his tags rattling like Christmas bells. He clawed her arm as she found the buckle and slid it loose. The collar fell to the floor. Ritchie flew across the room, snarling.

Buddy Holly sang that love was love and wouldn't fade away as Alma fell forward on her hands and Ritchie landed on the back of the couch, lashing his tail. *"De nada!"* Alma called after him. Already, long red welts rose where his claws had raked her skin.

But it wasn't Ritchie's fault he didn't realize she had helped him. He was only a cat and didn't know any better.

Not like people, who should know that it was wrong to run with gangs and deal coke.

That it was wrong to break into other people's houses.

Alma shied away from that last thought. This wasn't the same. It didn't hurt anyone. Besides, if she hadn't been here, Ritchie might have hurt himself fighting free of the collar. She'd done Mrs. B. a favor and earned her right to be here.

Her stomach rumbled. It was late. She hadn't had much breakfast.

But Alma didn't want to go back to that house, where everyone was angry, where there was no music, no Abuela, nothing but work and yelling and more work.

And nothing she'd done for Ritchie would entitle her to raid Mrs. B.'s pantry. Alma knew better than that!

- 14 -

the *blame*

Lunchtime came and went. Alma looked in the refrigerator, in the bread box, in the bear-shaped cookie jar. Would Mrs. B. really miss one vanilla wafer, one slice of bread with butter?

It didn't matter whether she missed them or not. Alma wasn't about to steal her food. But she couldn't go back, either. She put her head into the sink to drink out of the faucet and wandered around the house. The pictures in the hall smiled at her. When she stared at the faces long enough, Alma could see that the girl at the piano was Mrs. B. It was harder to find the Mr. B. she remembered—the bald spot, the wide belly—in the scrawny, shaggy boy with the guitar, but who else could it be? He smiled at her, as if about to tell a joke.

Mrs. B. had a hall closet, too, with a heavy brass knob and big, old-fashioned keyhole—as if anybody anywhere had ever locked a closet! If Eddie'd been able to lock his closet, the coke would still be there, and she would still be happy. Mrs. B.'s closet held a winter coat, two pairs of boots, a couple of men's suits in dry cleaner bags, and a guitar case that looked brand-new. Alma touched it, wondering if this was a special guitar, for playing at dances or concerts, wondering if it would sound different than the everyday one in the living room. She fingered the latch, put it back, shut the closet door.

The changer used up all the music in it, so Alma put on an Ella Fitzgerald disc, then took another stab at playing the everyday guitar. She could play "Three Blind Mice" and "Mary Had a Little Lamb" pretty well by now, but there was no satisfaction in such baby tunes. She tried playing *La bamba* by ear, but if she played fast enough, she hit the wrong notes; if she slowed down enough to get the notes right, it was impossible to dance to. Faintly from outside, Alma heard Lalo's car get back, then Mama's.

She looked at the clock and decided she could stay a little longer. She didn't want to be in the house when Mama found out what had happened.

Ritchie avoided her. Bopper let himself out. Buddy let himself in and demanded serious petting, so she worked on him until she heard a car engine cut off out front and realized that Mrs. B. was home. She dumped Buddy off her lap with a hasty "Sorry!" and ran. She heard Mrs. B.'s feet on the front porch as she opened the back door. No time to bolt it again! She ran out, barely remembering to catch the screen door before it slammed, and hurled herself over the fence, her hair slapping her back like a hand pushing her onward.

Rosalia was just putting down the phone in the kitchen as Alma came in. "Where have you been?" she yelled.

Lalo and Mama ran in as Alma stepped back. Moving with unexpected speed, Mama caught her before she could run out again. "Don't *ever* do that!" she shouted, shaking Alma.

"What are you yelling at *me* for?" Alma shouted back. "I'm not the drug dealer!"

Lalo jerked her out of Mama's grip, which at least stopped the shaking. "No, you're a runaway," he said sternly, but not shouting. "We were scared stiff. For all we knew, you'd been kidnapped or hit by a car. Where were you?"

Alma looked at her feet. "Out."

"Out where?" snapped Mama.

"I don't know!" The lie tumbled out of her mouth before she knew it was there, and she hurried on to the truth. "I didn't want to be here with all the yelling." She glared around at each of them. "Where's Eddie?"

Mama plopped into the nearest chair and started crying. Rosalia leaped up to hug her. Lalo looked grim.

Alma felt sick. "Did the police come get him?"

"No," said Rosalia. "We didn't call the police."

"But we told him that we would the next time he screwed up like this," said Lalo, "and he'd have to tell on his Chupacabras buddies or go to juvenile hall. He stormed out."

"He hit Lalo!" Rosalia interrupted.

"Only after I hit him." Lalo felt his jaw. "I should've known better. But I lost it!"

"Wh-where's the coke?" asked Alma.

"We flushed it," said Rosalia. "It was the only thing to do."

All this time Mama rocked back and forth in her chair, crying softly and steadily as a leaking faucet. "It's my fault," she said. "I'm a horrible mother. First my big girl gets pregnant and leaves school, then my boy's a criminal, and who knows what Alma's going to do in a year or two!"

"Mama, no!" exclaimed Lalo.

Rosalia started crying, too.

Alma slipped into the living room, where Silvita, innocent as a cat, chewed her stuffed dog in her playpen. Glumly, she took Silvita out and wondered if Mama was right. Maybe she'd think Alma's going next door made her a criminal. Well, it didn't! Bringing drugs into the house was lots worse than anything she'd ever done.

But it wasn't necessarily worse than anything she was ever going to do.

Would Silvita grow up to make huge mistakes, too?

Rosalia heated canned spaghetti and threw a salad together for supper. "We'll have to send him to Manuel's when he comes back," Mama said, poking at a tomato.

"He won't stay there," predicted Lalo.

"It's the only thing we can do," Rosalia said. "We can't have him bringing stuff like that into the same house with Alma and Silvita."

Alma, hungry and queasy at the same time, tried to eat but couldn't. Instead she bent over her plate, moving spaghetti around, tucking her hair behind her ears to keep it out of the spaghetti sauce.

What had happened to her ponytail? Where was her scrunch?

Had she lost it going in through the cat door? Or coming out? Or going over the fence? Or—*ay!* Had she lost it in the house?

She'd left Ella Fitzgerald in the changer.

And she hadn't locked the back door.

What would Mrs. B. think when she found her house like that? Would she come next door and ask her neighbors if they'd seen someone hanging around?

Would she dig the scrunch out of the couch cushions and know a girl with long hair had been there?

Mama got off to work late, not crying anymore but looking as patient and miserable as a sick animal. "Call me if he comes," she said on her way out the door.

But he didn't come, not that night, or the next, or the next.

And Mrs. B. did not come over.

Alma was grounded for staying out all day without saying where she was going. It could have been so much worse that she didn't complain but looked after Silvita as sweetly as she could. Rosalia did some serious job hunting while Alma baby-sat, but even on Friday, when she ran out of leads, she wouldn't let Alma, who was getting antsy for relief, go farther than the yard. Alma practiced her fingering on air, feeling her little bit of hard-won skill leaking out from lack of practice. She forgot all about it, though, when Silvita, shouting proudly, waddled upright from the playpen to the couch. Alma and Rosalia took turns laughing and hugging her and got her to walk back and forth between the two of them for half an hour before she wore out and got cranky.

On Saturday, the police found the owner of the gun that had killed Jovita. He claimed it had been stolen out of his pickup a week before the drive by, but he hadn't reported the theft, so no one believed him. He appeared on TV with his face blurred out by the news camera, explaining and explaining. "I thought I knew who took it," he said. "And I thought I could handle it. By the time I found out I was wrong, it'd been so long, I thought it wasn't worth the hassle. If I'd known you'd come harassing me and my family about some ex-gang singer, I'd've done different, but we didn't have nothing to do with it, so you can just leave me alone."

"I wonder which of his family did it," remarked Rosalia.

"He could be telling the truth," suggested Lalo.

"But he isn't," said Alma. "I wish they'd show his face! I'd find him and *make* him tell me!"

"That's why they didn't show his face," said Lalo. "This guy and his whole family are innocent till proved guilty, and anybody that tries to take them down's as bad as the ones that killed Jovita."

Alma wasn't so sure of this, but she didn't argue. A new song was playing in the back of her head. An angry song, for Jovita and her killer, and Eddie, and everybody whose family did things that everybody else had to live with. She could feel it, thumping in her brain, but couldn't hear it well enough to even hum it. Not in this house.

She needed quiet, and a guitar. She needed Mrs. B.'s house.

- 15 -

the confession

The weekend passed, and Monday, and Tuesday. Once Buddy came over while Alma had Silvita in the backyard, and she introduced them to each other, wondering if she dared go to Mrs. B.'s with Silvita in tow. But though Buddy was his usual friendly self, Silvita couldn't be convinced that there was any difference between him and her stuffed dog, whose ears she habitually chewed. The introduction ended in scratching, indignation, and hollering all around. Buddy streaked for the door with his fur puffed up. Alma took Silvita inside and washed the scratch, which wasn't nearly as bad as her own from Ritchie had been. Then she turned on the radio and danced Silvita around the room till she giggled and was happy again.

They danced to La Mafia and to Emilio, and then the DJ came on, talking excitedly. "I just heard a rumor," he said, "that Jovita's killer has confessed!"

Alma stopped dead in the middle of the floor.

"This is just a rumor," said the DJ, "but I heard it from one of the newsroom folks. I don't know anything yet. Maybe it's some crazy that wants to be famous, or maybe it's an accusation instead of a confession, I don't know. But as soon as we do know, I'll tell you, so keep your radios right here. Meantime, let's listen to her!" He started playing *En mi corazón.*

Silvita pulled hard on her hair, and Alma sat down on the floor. "Confessed," she said to Silvita. "Why would anybody confess? Unless they feel real bad. Unless they're sorry."

But this wasn't the sort of thing you could fix by saying "Sorry!"

"*Ay!*"

Silvita yanked at Alma's hair, giggling. Alma lightly shook her. "Stop that! It hurts!"

Silvita's face wobbled.

Alma hugged her and gently untangled her fist.

She left the radio on all day, playing with Silvita, putting her down for her nap, and getting her up again, and the DJ kept repeating the rumor and never saying anything for sure. Rosalia came back for lunch and then went out on an interview—a real interview, not just applying—that took her so long, Lalo came home from school before she got back.

He was coaxing Silvita to walk to him, and Alma was telling him about the rumor, when the DJ came on again. She stopped talking so he could hear for himself.

"It's official!" the DJ said, breathless and ragged, as if he were laughing, or crying, or maybe both at once. "It's kind of a confession and kind of an accusation. It was gangs, like we didn't know that already! The younger sister of one of Las Princesas has admitted to being in the car with her sister and two other girls. They were doing a drive by on the house where the old woman and the little boy were hit, trying to get one of Las Howling Madres. So far we don't have any names, but the police have everyone involved in custody. The sister says she came forward because keeping the secret was wrecking her whole family. She couldn't stand it that her own father was telling lies about the gun."

The DJ talked faster and faster. Alma felt herself shaking, the way she shook in PE right before she had to let go of the chin-up bar.

"Yes, both these girls are the daughters of the guy we all saw last week claiming his gun had been stolen before it was used to kill Jovita." The DJ's voice cracked. "Not that anybody believed that!"

"Told you," said Alma to Lalo.

"I can't—I can't talk about this anymore," said the DJ. "Later. I need to pull myself together. After we hear this song." He put on the *"Jovita polkita."*

"That poor kid," said Lalo, rubbing Silvita's head.

"Poor kid? She should've told right away!" declared Alma.

"Oh, you think so? What if you'd known Eddie had done it? Or Rosalia? Or me?"

"You wouldn't do anything like this," said Alma. "Even Eddie wouldn't."

"Oh, no?" Lalo carried Silvita over to the refrigerator and got out a bottle of soda.

"Of course not!"

"A week ago, would you've said Eddie'd bring drugs home?"

"That's different."

"Not much." Lalo put ice into two glasses. "And what if Eddie was in the car and didn't know it was going to happen till it did?" He poured soda over the ice. "Nobody knows what they'd do till they do it."

"*I* know!" declared Alma. "I wouldn't hang with a gang, ever!"

"So you're walking along with Maggie," said Lalo, putting the cap back on the soda. "And a car comes by with folks she knows but you don't, and they offer you a ride, and she says yes. Wouldn't you get in the car, too?"

"Well, sure," said Alma. "But—"

"And what if after you got in, you saw gang colors?"

"I'd get out!"

"Even if Maggie says it's okay, don't be chicken?" He slid one of the sodas over to her.

Alma took the glass and didn't say anything. At times like this, she could sort of see why Eddie didn't like Lalo. He talked too much.

"And what if one of them points a gun at you and says: 'Here, hold this'?"

"I—I wouldn't."

"Even if he bumps you with it and you think maybe he's a little drunk?"

"Look, none of this will ever happen to me. My friends don't want to be in gangs!"

"None of the friends you have now," said Lalo, "but when you go to middle school, there'll be lots of new people. And some of them will be from neighborhoods where if you're not in a gang you're beat up every day. They might act like good kids at school, and then when they go home they don't have a choice anymore. It happens." He frowned into his soda. "For all you know, this kid that confessed is like that. For all we know, her sister killed Jovita because she was trying *not* to hit the house they were shooting at. She's probably old enough to be tried as an adult, and she could get death."

"She *deserves it*," said Alma, but she couldn't look at him as she said it.

"Maybe," said Lalo. "Maybe Eddie deserved to go to jail. You wish we'd called the police on him?" He finally drank some of his soda. Alma couldn't think of anything to say. "Just be glad it wasn't you or me," he said.

But Alma didn't think she would ever be glad about anything.

- 16 -

the return

At last, after a week and a half, Rosalia declared a day off from job hunting, but even so, it didn't look as if Alma could get out of the house. "You haven't done a lick of work all the time you've been home," declared Rosalia. "You can help me do laundry."

"I've been working!" protested Alma. "I baby-sat Silvita, and I washed dishes, and I made lunch for her and me, and—"

"And you let the dirty clothes pile up and didn't make your bed, and look how filthy the floor is," interrupted Rosalia. "Come on, pitch in!"

This was so unfair that Alma nearly broke her jaw grinding her teeth, but she went through the house picking up dirty clothes (she was *not* the only one leaving clothes lying around!) and stripping beds. Rosalia vacuumed the living room, and Alma picked Silvita's toys off the floors while a load of permanent press washed on the back porch. Alma didn't see the point of not being grounded anymore if she was stuck doing housework, and she didn't see the point of Rosalia being home with Silvita if Rosalia was vacuuming in the living room and Silvita was in her crib. Alma's new song tapped at the front of her skull and twitched in her fingers, trying to get out. The song had gotten steadily stronger since she heard about the confession, until she could almost hum it and could tap out the rhythm on Silvita's xylophone.

The confessing girl had been on the news last night, and Alma recognized her as one of the neighbors interviewed at the time of the death, the one who had said it must've been an accident. That was going into the song, but she wasn't sure where yet; maybe part of the chorus. An accident, an accident. How much of an accident was it if you set out to kill people and wound up killing the wrong ones? How could she make this big idea short enough to fit the half-heard music in her head?

The unbalanced washing machine shook the house on the spin cycle, making Silvita's crib skitter on its casters. The vacuum cleaner stopped roaring. Alma, dropping plastic doughnuts into the toy box, heard Rosalia putting it away and a murmur of radio. Suddenly the house stopped shaking as the cycle ended. "Come help me hang out the clothes," called Rosalia.

"When are we getting the dryer fixed?" called Alma, checking to make sure the side of the crib was fastened securely.

"We don't need a dryer in the summer. It'd just make the house hotter. Come on and stop whining!"

"I wasn't whining!" Alma protested, stamping through the kitchen on her way to the back porch. "I was asking. Why are you so crabby, anyhow?"

"This might be the last day I get to stay home," said Rosalia. "They said they'd call this afternoon about the job."

This made it even more urgent to get next door. "That shouldn't make you crabby," said Alma. "You should be glad you can start earning money."

"I am, I guess, but I don't want to work for a cleaning service," grumbled Rosalia, opening the washing machine lid.

"Then you should have stayed in school and learned to be a computer geek or something," said Alma, helping her drag out the twisted rope of sheets, shirts, and blouses.

"Oh, don't you start! You sound like Lalo."

"There's worse people to sound like."

"Lalo isn't any fun anymore, and if I do like he wants me to, I won't ever have any fun again."

"Sure, you will," said Alma, her stomach feeling as if she were going down in an elevator. "When he gets out of school and finds a good job—"

"Then we'll have to pay off his student loan, and we're still not done paying for the hospital where Silvita was born."

"I thought Mama was paying for that."

"Mama's still paying for Abuela's funeral, and our clothes, and our food, and rent, and—" Rosalia groaned, hefting the laundry basket. "Oh, never mind. I'm sorry. Being a grown-up makes you crabby, that's all. I couldn't wait to be one, but now I'm here and I wish I wasn't."

"When I'm a grown-up—" Alma began, but a slam at the front of the house interrupted her. She and Rosalia looked at each other.

"Eddie," said Rosalia, only half out loud.

Alma's heart thudded; with relief or dismay, she couldn't tell which. Rosalia shoved the full laundry basket at her, and she took it, unthinking.

"You hang this stuff up," said Rosalia, "and I'll go talk to him."

Alma looked over her shoulder on her way to the clothesline, but the kitchen window only showed her the bedraggled begonia over the sink and the color of the refrigerator. She unwound Lalo's Sunday shirt from a sheet and hung it up by the hem, a clothespin at each seam. She hung a flowered pillowcase, and Rosalia's green cotton dress, and Silvita's yellow crib sheet.

The shouting started inside.

Shouting and banging around. It came closer, retreated, came closer again. Sweat rolling down the front of her tank top, Alma hung up sheets and pillowcases and T-shirts, glancing toward the kitchen window. Shadows passed between the begonia and the refrigerator. She couldn't make out the words, but there were three voices. Eddie had brought Tino home with him. Alma hung up her red shorts and struggled with the flowered sheets from Lalo and Rosalia's bed, sweating, thinking longingly of the cool, quiet dimness of Mrs. B.'s house.

"Get out, get out, get out!" yelled Rosalia.

Silvita started crying.

Alma hung up the last pillowcase and bent over the laundry basket, breathing hard. She should go in and back up Rosalia, or hush Silvita, or something. But she didn't want to see Eddie, she didn't want to meet Tino, she didn't want to be dragged into the fight, and she felt as though she'd been looking after Silvita every day of her life.

The radio turned on, loud as a jackhammer, drowning out Rosalia and Silvita, too. Alma scrambled over the fence, strode across the yard, took the four porch steps in two strides, scratched herself on the screen undoing the latch. Ritchie, curled up underneath the porch chair, awoke with a start and hissed at her, but she ignored him, thrust her upper body through the cat door, and strained for the bolt. It shot back with a satisfying *thunk,* barely audible as the radio next door switched from *tejano* to rap. Alma stood up and twisted the doorknob.

The rap music beat on the edges of the house's quiet when she pulled the door shut behind her, but the quiet here wasn't just a matter of sound. It was a matter of coolness, of emptiness, of no human presence but her own. Alma took a deep breath of quiet and padded across the kitchen. Buddy, curled up in the kitchen sink, sat up and meowed. "Hey, Buddy," said Alma, stopping to rub his head, feeling the sickness in her stomach and the tightness in her chest begin to drain away.

"Puh-rrp," said Buddy. Then he tensed under her hand and turned his head, yellow ears swiveling alertly, at the sound of heavy footsteps shaking the back porch.

- 17 -

the break-in

The rap music stopped. Alma blinked. "I'm sure I saw her," said Eddie, outside. "Look, the screen door's not latched."

"Yeah, but she couldn't fit through the cat door," said Tino. "She's not that skinny."

"Then the door must not be locked," said Eddie. "Man, my little sister, a burglar!"

"You're letting her get ahead of you, man!"

Rowr!

"Stupid cat!"

Thump, bang, *hiss!*

The doorknob turned.

Alma looked around for a place to hide, but the kitchen was tidy and shadowless, and her body and brain seemed to have shut off like the radio. Before she could lift her hand from Buddy's back, he had climbed onto the counter, watching the door, his tail jerking back and forth. She could retreat through the dining room and out the front door—but the back door was already open, Tino and Eddie pushing through, bringing with them a smell of stale beer and cigarettes. They blinked in the dimness, but they saw her, all right. Eddie laughed. *"Hola, hermanita!* You miss me?"

"No!" said Alma. "Get out of here!"

Tino strode into the kitchen. "Oh, this is your house now, huh? Hey, it's real nice. You got anything to eat? My old man ran out of food. That's why we came back here." He pulled the lid off the cookie jar.

"Yeah, but Rosalia's being a witch," said Eddie, "and she chased us out of the kitchen with a broom. Can you believe it?"

Tino stuffed vanilla wafers into his mouth, scattering crumbs when he bit. Buddy walked toward him, stiff legged. "Ooh, an attack cat!" Tino laughed, swiping at him with one hand.

Buddy dodged. Alma darted forward. "Leave the cats alone!" she yelled, slapping his hands. "And get out of their house!"

Tino hit her with the back of his hand, right across the cheek. Alma, caught off balance, staggered back. "Hey, don't hurt my little sister," said Eddie casually. "That's my job."

Buddy jumped off the counter and streaked out through the back door. Alma stamped her feet, tears burning the backs of her eyes. "Get out! Get out!"

"Why?" asked Eddie. "'Cause you got here first? There's plenty here for everybody."

"So, have you had time to look around?" asked Tino through a mouthful of vanilla wafer. "Where's the old bag keep her jewelry?"

Alma stared at him. There was a jewelry box in the bedroom, full of earrings and necklaces and some cuff links. "You're not—you wouldn't—you can't steal from Mrs. B.!"

"Stop trying to act like a goody two-shoes," said Eddie. "We think it was real smart of you to figure out how to break in here. We won't tell, will we, Tino?"

Tino shook his head and crossed his heart.

"It's not like that! I didn't come here to steal things."

"Oh, yeah," said Tino. "You came to play with the cute little kitty cats, right? Shove her outside, Eddie; she's getting on my nerves."

"Naw," said Eddie. "We wouldn't have got in here

without her. Not without breaking something. She deserves a fair share."

"I don't want a share of anything!"

"Well, you can't have it all yourself," said Eddie, with patient reasonableness. "You don't even know what to take or where to get rid of it."

Alma trembled all over. "I've never taken anything, *nada*! I just listen to the stereo and play the guitar and I leave! I even put her CDs back the way they were!"

"Never?" said Eddie. "What do you mean, 'never'? How often you been here?"

"What difference does it make? I never took anything. I'm not a thief!"

"Sure, you are," said Eddie. "If you listen to her stereo and play her guitar, you're a music thief."

"A stereo and a guitar, huh?" said Tino. "That's a good place to start. Come on!" He headed toward the front of the house, through the dining room.

"No!" Alma ran around in front of him. "You can't take Mrs. B.'s stuff!"

"Watch me." Tino shoved her aside and nearly tripped on Bopper, sprawled inside the dining-room door. "How many cats does this old lady have?" He drew back his foot.

Alma kicked him. "You leave Bopper alone!"

Tino grabbed her as Bopper ran toward the living room. Alma squealed as Tino twisted her arm around behind her back and shook her. "Listen, runt, you help or you keep out of the way! Or else!"

"Tino!" snapped Eddie.

"Hey, you don't want me whaling on your sister, you keep her in line," said Tino, letting go of Alma and stalking into the living room.

Eddie bent over Alma. "What's up with you? An old lady like Mrs. B.'s bound to have lots of good stuff. You can buy yourself a new tape deck, and then you won't have to come over here for music."

"It's *stealing*." Eddie was looking at her almost like the brother she used to have. Maybe he would listen to her.

"So?"

"So it's wrong!"

"Oh, don't give me that!"

Alma was trying so hard not to cry, she could hardly breathe, much less talk. "You'll get caught, and you'll go to juvenile hall, and—"

"And so will you." Eddie grabbed her wrist and put his face down close to hers. "If you're thinking of telling on us, you better think again. 'Cause if I hadn't seen you go over the fence, we never would've come into this yard, and if you hadn't already gone inside, we never would have thought the door was open. And you're the one breaking and entering, not us!"

"It's n-not like that—"

"You think the judge'll believe you never took anything? You'll have a rap sheet, and everybody'll know you're a no-good kid, and you'll never get a job and you'll have to steal to live. What'd'you think of *that*, Miss Goody Two-Shoes?"

Alma could only stare at him.

"Hey, Eddie, check it out!" called Tino. "This old lady's got some primo equipment! We're gonna need a truck!"

Eddie let go of Alma and went to the living room. "Everybody'd see a truck."

"Not if we brought it up the alley," said Tino.

Their voices faded out in the roaring in Alma's ears. She let the tears spill out now; why not? Everything was ruined. Eddie was right—she was a music thief, and if she told on Eddie and Tino, she'd get arrested the same as they would.

Bopper slipped through the other door, having gone out of the living room through the hall. He turned his fluffy face toward her and mouthed a reproachful "meow" before trotting toward the still-open back door.

If she didn't tell on Eddie and Tino, Mrs. B. would lose all her nice stuff, and the house would be ruined. No more quiet, no more peace, no more music pouring out of the walls.

Why should she care? She could never come back, anyway.

Alma balled up her fists and ran after Bopper, whose fluffy tail, twice its usual size, was disappearing through the tear in the screen porch. The fence shook noisily as she hauled herself over it, and she sobbed as she stumbled into Rosalia, coming out with a load of towels.

"Alma, what the heck—?"

Alma pushed past her and ran to the phone. The dial tone droned in her ear until she hit the nine button, then it fell silent.

"Alma, what's going on? Why are you crying?"

One, one. Ring.

Alma held up a finger for Rosalia to wait and sniffed, listening for the operator. "Nine-one-one emergency," said the voice on the other end.

"My brother is robbing my next-door neighbor," said Alma. "You better send the police."

- 18 -

the consequences

The arrest did not go well. The boys must have heard the police car arrive, because they ran out the back and into the alley. The cops caught Tino, who wouldn't let go of Mrs. B.'s CD player, but Eddie dropped her big tape deck and took off across the yard. The tape deck was broken, and it and the CD player were both confiscated as evidence.

The cops wouldn't listen to Alma or to Tino when they tried to distribute blame fairly. Even the one who stayed around to get all the details after Tino took off in the police car didn't seem as interested as he should be. "You did the right thing, calling us," he said. "I know it wasn't easy, turning in your own brother."

"But it was my fault, too," Alma said wearily. "I broke in. He just followed me."

"He's older than you," said the police officer. "He knew better."

"So did I!"

The police officer watched Lalo's car pull up, watched him climb out looking grim. "You turned state's evidence. I don't have to arrest you. And I'm sure your folks will see to it you suffer, if that's what you want," he told Alma.

But there was so much talking and shouting and asking questions that nobody seemed to have time to be mad at Alma. After Mama arrived and Alma had told her story for the fourth time, people stopped even asking her questions. Rosalia dug through Eddie's closet, looking for Tino's phone number, to call his dad, and Lalo and Mama talked to the police officer about what would happen to Eddie now. Alma went back to her room, where Silvita fussed to be taken out of her crib. Alma ignored her and opened her backpack. Her tapes were still there, where she'd left them.

"Aaalma," whined Silvita.

Alma turned. "Did you say my name? Did you talk?"

Silvita reached her arms over the side of the crib and wrinkled up her face. "Al-ma-maal-maal-maal."

Maybe it was talking, and maybe it wasn't. Alma hooked the backpack over one arm, scooped up her niece, and went out on the front porch to wait.

When Mrs. B. came up, the police officer met her at the car, and they went into the house together. Rosalia, Lalo, and Mama clustered on the front porch, talking about lawyers and juvenile hall and Tío Manuel. Alma watched Mrs. B.'s door, rocking Silvita back and forth and singing to her. She sang, "Not Anymore" and the song she had worked so hard on but would never finish now, and *"En mi corazón."* Mama cried, and Rosalia took her inside. Lalo sat down beside her.

"I'm sorry," said Alma, resting her chin on Silvita's soft hair.

"I'm not the one you have to apologize to," said Lalo.

"I know," said Alma. "But I'm sorry, anyway."

When the police officer drove away, Alma gave Silvita to Lalo and crossed the yards with her eyes down. Mrs. B.'s grass was thin and sparse and dry; it wasn't being watered enough. The monkey grass along the front sidewalk was getting mixed up with runners of the regular grass, and the flower bed along the front porch had no flowers in it, only the dry stalks of something that had died back and not been replaced. She walked up Mrs. B.'s steps one at a time, the tapes inside the backpack slapping her leg, and rang the bell.

She heard movement inside. Buddy, appearing from under the porch, trotted over to rub against her legs. Alma was bending to pet him when the door opened. She looked up at Mrs. B., with her gray-blond hair straggling out of its neat braid, her eyes puffy, her nose red, and her crisp white blouse coming out in the back.

Alma took a deep breath and started talking, fast, in English. "I'm sorry. It was all my fault, and I shouldn't ever have done it." She almost dropped the backpack, digging the tapes out. "Only it was so noisy at home, and after Eddie took my tape deck I couldn't listen to my Jovita tapes, and then I found the guitar book and I wanted to learn, only none of that's any excuse and I know it. But I kept thinking if I wasn't taking anything out I wasn't hurting anything and it was all right." She thrust the tapes at her. "This is to show you how sorry I am. I know you don't have any, and I know you'll like it, and anyway, I don't de-deserve to have them and—and—I'm just sorry."

Mrs. B. stared at her, making no move to take the tapes. "Have you any idea," she said slowly, "how it feels to know that your house—your house that's your own special place—that people you don't even really know come strolling through it whenever they feel like?"

"Yes," said Alma. "No. I mean, I never had a special place except for . . . except for your house, and that wasn't mine, but when Eddie and Tino came in I felt sick. And you must feel about a thousand times worse. And I'm sorry." She put the tapes into Mrs. B.'s unresisting hand. "But that doesn't change anything." That seemed to be everything she could say, so she turned around and ran back home, past Lalo, into the living room, into her own room, where she buried her head under the pillow and wished she would smother, but didn't.

- 19 -

the answer

Three days later, while Mama was eating her early supper and Alma was feeding Silvita, the phone rang. Rosalia answered it, and her face changed. "Just a minute." She held it out, as if it were a snake. "Mama. The police. They found him."

Mama slowly pushed her chair back and got up. Alma wiped Silvita's face and took her outside to walk around the yard, letting go of her for a few minutes at a time so she could walk by herself, catching her hand again at the first sign of a wobble. She hummed a few bars of *"Duérmete, por favor,"* and stopped. She didn't want Silvita to sleep, and she didn't deserve to make songs.

Mrs. B.'s back door opened. Mrs. B. stepped over Ritchie, sunning himself on the back step, walked over to the fence, and said: "Evening, Alma."

Alma hung her head to watch Silvita pull herself along the fence by the diamond-shaped links. "Evening, ma'am."

Mrs. B. held out a hair scrunch, covered with fuzz and fur. "Buddy was playing with this on the back porch. Is it yours?"

"Um—yes, ma'am. Thank you." Alma took it and stuffed it into her pocket, not meeting her neighbor's eyes. "Um—the cops found Eddie. Mama's on the phone with them."

"You must have been very worried about him."

Alma looked at the ground. The funnels of doodlebug nests dotted the bare dirt.

"I listened to those tapes on my portable," Mrs. B. said, almost as if nothing was wrong. Almost. "My Spanish is pretty bad, but this Jovita has—had—a marvelous voice. And once I got used to the music, I could tell it was good, too. Did she play her own instruments?"

Alma had to swallow before she could talk around the dryness in her mouth. "She played guitar and accordion."

"And what about—what about you?" asked Mrs. B. "You said you wanted to learn guitar in my house. What was that about?"

"I found that guitar and the teaching books," Alma said, "and I tried to teach myself. I wasn't very good. I could sort of play 'Mary Had a Little Lamb' and 'Three Blind Mice.' But I couldn't play real songs. I kind of know how to play the recorder, from school, but I never touched yours, I promise."

"You—went into my bedroom?" For a minute, she sounded about to cry; then her voice went even again. "Of course you did. Why wouldn't you, once you were in?"

"I kept my hands behind my back. So I wouldn't touch anything."

"You must have come in a lot, to manage even 'Three Blind Mice' without a teacher," said Mrs. B.

"I guess. I came every day I could. Since Jovita died."

"Which was, what? Six weeks ago?"

Alma shrugged. Since it shouldn't have happened at all, she didn't see that it mattered how often she'd done it. Too often—and not enough.

"That guitar belonged to my husband," Mrs. B. said. "The books, too. He tried to teach me guitar, but I never took to it like some people do. It takes tough fingers. Anton had calluses on his fingers from the strings and the picks."

Alma picked at the lump of hard yellow skin that had begun to form on the edge of her thumb and said nothing.

"Why did you first come into my house?" asked Mrs. B.

"Jovita died," said Alma. A mockingbird sang in the stillness after her voice stopped; Silvita worked her way along the fence, rattling the links; Mrs. B. waited. "I didn't plan it. I was—I felt so—" She stopped, intimidated by the size of the feeling, the first huge and terrible feeling of this huge and terrible summer. "Buddy and Bopper showed me how to get in. It was almost like they were inviting me." The story dribbled out, little bit by little bit: how she had started, how she had continued. Mrs. B. kept on not saying anything, and Alma almost forgot, in the interest of describing her song, to feel bad and hesitant and nervous. But she remembered again as soon as she stopped.

"You were making a song?" Mrs. B. sounded interested—almost pleased. "Can you sing it?"

"Well—it's in Spanglish. It's about trying to get the baby to sleep." She sang the chorus, her hips automatically twitching, and Silvita echoed the rhythm:

"Beh-beh-beh-beh," before sitting down on the ground and tearing up fistfuls of grass.

"That's not bad, for a kid," said Mrs. B. "Am I hearing an echo of the Supremes in there?"

"Yes, ma'am." Alma knelt over Silvita, eyes open in case she tried to eat dirt. "Why are you being nice to me? I don't deserve it."

"I don't deserve to hate the kid next door," said Mrs. B. "I did hate you, for a while. But then I wondered what made you call the police on your own brother. And how long you'd been coming without my noticing. You were good at putting things back—I only ever found the door unlocked or the wrong CD in the player once, and even then I thought I must have been forgetful. I never suspected anything wrong. And you seemed like such a nice girl, always looking after the baby, always polite to me—and the cats."

"Well, now you know better."

"I know you made a mistake, and I know you're sorry, and I know your family has enough troubles without my making them worse."

"Does that mean you're not going to prosecute Eddie?" The question popped out before Alma could stop herself.

"No," said Mrs. B., "but he'll probably only get probation, anyway. It wasn't his idea, and he didn't get away with anything. Probation ought to be harsh enough. I don't think punishing people does much good, you know. If every time a piano student makes a mistake, you slap his hand, he makes more and more mistakes. But if you make him understand what the mistake was, he'll improve."

That made Alma think of the girls who had killed Jovita, but that was too enormous to think about right now. "So what are you going to do?" she asked.

"I don't know," said Mrs. B. "If I knew how to make a kid like Eddie understand his mistakes, I'd quit piano and go into social work." She smiled, without looking any less sad. "But I'm getting myself a burglar alarm and fixing the screen, so as not to put temptation in anybody else's way."

"That's a good idea." Alma sighed. "But then Buddy and Bopper and Ritchie won't be able to go in and out."

"They'll just have to live with that," said Mrs. B. "Um—did you ever play records by the people I named them after? Ritchie Valens and the Big Bopper and Buddy Holly?"

"Sure, sometimes," said Alma.

"They died, like Jovita," said Mrs. B., looking down at Silvita.

"What, *all* of them?" Alma squeaked.

"All on the same night," said Mrs. B. "In 1958. They were touring in a small plane, and it went down, and they all died. In Iowa. It seemed so impossible. Buddy—Buddy Holly just about invented rock and roll, churned out song after song after song for two years, and then suddenly he—wasn't there. It was like—it was like—" She spread her hands. "My mother thought I was crazy, mourning so hard for three men that had never been anything to me but voices on the radio. Maybe I was a little crazy for a while. I did things I never would have done before that time, and it's hard now for me to believe I ever did them."

Alma pricked up her ears. "What did you do?"

"I'm not telling!" Mrs. B. laughed shakily. "It's too embarrassing!"

"I hate death!" Alma blurted out.

"So do I. When Anton died, I couldn't think, couldn't play music, couldn't do anything but sit and know that he wasn't here anymore."

"When Abuela—when my grandmother died, everybody said it was a blessing in disguise, because she had cancer and hurt all the time," said Alma, her voice wobbling. "But it didn't feel like a blessing. Not to me."

"People told me I should be glad Anton died quickly and didn't live with a lot of pain," said Mrs. B., her voice also wobbling. "I wanted to scream at them. He was my husband, and I had a right to feel bad that he wasn't here anymore!"

Silvita grabbed Alma's leg to steady herself as she stood up. Alma stood over her, listening to the mockingbird, watching her, so small, frowning with the effort of standing. She didn't know what to say to Mrs. B., but the sick, heavy feeling in her head and stomach was lighter than it had been in a long time.

Mrs. B. shifted her weight. "How old are you?"

"Eleven," said Alma. "Why?"

"I need a kid to do my yard work. But I suppose you're a little young for it still."

"Twelve-year-olds do yards," said Alma. "I could do it next year. Would you—would you want *me* doing your yard?"

"I might, in a while." Mrs. B. smiled at her, a thin, determined sort of smile. "Give me time. I might even want to teach you some music. You ought to finish your song. But that's not a promise, and I can't teach guitar."

If she wasn't going to bear grudges, the least Alma could do was to let her. She smiled back. "Piano and recorder are good, too."

Inside, they were discussing what to do about Eddie while Mama got her stuff together for her night job. "It won't hurt him to sit there overnight," said Mama. "I'll go down in the morning."

"I can do that for you, Mama," offered Lalo.

Mama shook her head. "No, but you can call Manuel for me."

In the living room, Rosalia flipped through the day's mail, bills and flyers and catalogs full of things that no real person could afford to buy. She held out a cream-colored envelope. "Hey, Alma. You got a letter."

"Me?" Alma never got letters, and this was typed and everything. She looked at the return address. *Lourdes Ramos de Aguilar.*

Alma sat down on the floor and tore open the top of the envelope, afraid to breathe. There was a folded-up piece of paper inside, and when she unfolded it, a smaller piece fell out, with handwriting all over it. *Jovita always answered her fan mail on her computer in the evening the same day she got it,* said the handwriting. *She started a bunch of letters printing and went out for her last walk, and we let them sit there until finally, this past week, we woke up enough to clean out her office. Thank you for writing to my girl and letting her know how much she was loved, before it was too late.*

"What is it?" asked Rosalia, but Alma barely heard her through the music in her head. She laid the letter flat and smoothed it out with her hand.

Dear Alma,

Thank you for writing to me. I always like to hear that I have made people happy. It must be hard for you to be happy with your grandmother gone, but next time I sing "La florita" I will sing it for her. Your brother-in-law is right. If you work hard enough, anything is possible, though sometimes you'll think the work is too hard and nothing seems possible at all. Only people who work straight through those times get where they want to go.

If you can't learn to play an instrument at school, you can at least join a choir. Our community center has a plan for teaching music to children who can't afford lessons. Maybe something like that will happen for you. And whether or not you ever get good enough to lead a band, music will always be good to you. I wish I had known what I wanted to do as early as you do. I could have avoided lots of mistakes and unhappiness.

You are the future. Be good and sing true.

Your friend,

Jovita

Alma closed her eyes, trembling all over. *I don't deserve this,* she thought.

But maybe, maybe, she could live up to it.